FERALS
THE SWARM DESCENDS

Also available:

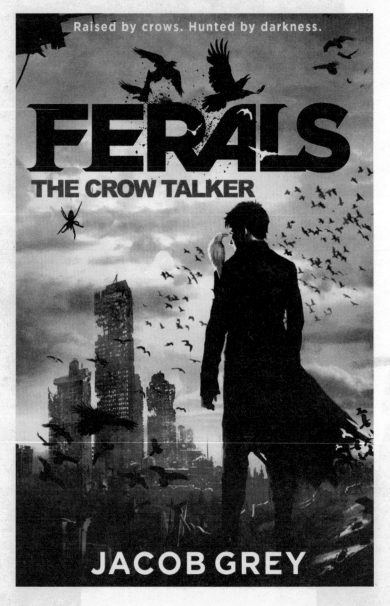

Raised by crows. Hunted by darkness.

FERALS
THE CROW TALKER

JACOB GREY

FERALS
THE SWARM DESCENDS

JACOB GREY

HarperCollins *Children's Books*

With special thanks to Michael Ford

First published in Great Britain by HarperCollins *Children's Books* 2015
HarperCollins *Children's Books* is a division of HarperCollins*Publishers* Ltd,
HarperCollins Publishers
1 London Bridge Street
London SE1 9GF

The HarperCollins *Children's Books* website address is
www.harpercollins.co.uk

1

Ferals: The Swarm Descends
Text © Working Partners Ltd 2015

978-0-00-757854-2

Printed and bound in England by
Clays Ltd, St Ives plc

FSC™ is a non-profit international organisation established to promote
the responsible management of the world's forests. Products carrying the
FSC label are independently certified to assure consumers that they come
from forests that are managed to meet the social, economic and
ecological needs of present and future generations,
and other controlled sources.

Find out more about HarperCollins and the environment at
www.harpercollins.co.uk/green

Chapter 1

There are ghosts in this place, thought Caw. Perhaps not the kind that swooped through empty rooms, banging doors and howling, but sadder spirits. Sorrow lingered here, silent, and lost from the memories of the living.

He checked the watch Crumb had given him – 2am.

This is a bad idea, said Glum. He was perched on a branch ten feet above, beak resting in the thick plumage of his chest feathers. *I'm older than you. Why does no one ever listen to the voice of experience?*

"I did listen," said Caw. "I just chose to ignore you."

He tried to sound confident, but his mouth was dry as he crouched, shivering, in the bushes. The house in front of him was abandoned, its walls flaking and covered in graffiti. He counted two intact windows, while the rest were either cracked or boarded up. The front lawn was so overgrown there wasn't even a path to the door.

One of the trees that grew beside the house had blown over in a storm and its branches, which had crushed a section of the roof, now appeared to be growing into the building.

Home sweet home, muttered Screech, hopping nervously along Caw's shoulder. The young crow's claws pricked Caw's skin, even through the leather of his coat.

Home? thought Caw. It didn't feel like it. Not at all.

He searched his memories, but couldn't find this place among them. He'd been five years old when the crows had carried him away, and nothing about the building in front of him was familiar. Except the unsettling feeling of dread he felt as he looked at it; the same feeling he had in his dreams.

Not too late to go back to the church, Caw, said Glum. *We could have those leftover sweet potato pancakes from dinner. Besides, how do we even know this is the right place?*

"I just know," said Caw, feeling cold certainty in his gut.

A snap of fluttering wings sounded at his back and a third crow alighted on the ground. Wiry and sleek, she stabbed a slender beak into the earth and prised up a wriggling worm. The slimy creature squirmed and coiled as the crow tossed back her head and gobbled it down.

Hey, Shimmer! said Screech, puffing out his chest.

Coast's clear, the female crow said, loose crumbs of earth dropping from her beak. *What are you all waiting for?*

For this young man to see sense, said Glum. *To let history lie.*

Don't be such a killjoy, said Shimmer, stretching her wings. They were sheened with blues and reds like spilt oil on wet tarmac. *It took me four weeks to find this place. If Caw's not going in, I am.*

"Can you all stop talking about me as if I'm not here?" said Caw. For once, the crows ceased their bickering. It was a rare occurrence since Shimmer had joined the group. Crows were stubborn. They liked to argue, and they liked having the last word even more. All except Milky, the white crow that Caw had grown up with. In all the years in the nest, he'd spoken less than twenty words. Caw wished the old crow was still with them.

He stood up, stretching his lower back and casting a glance back along the street. None of the buildings in this part of town was inhabited any more. The families had all moved out when the jobs dried up after the Dark Summer – the secret war between ferals that had broken out eight years ago. A broken and rusted scooter lay in a gutter full of leaves, and below, in a tree in a front garden, hung a lopsided swing, its cords frayed.

Caw wondered for a moment what it had been like growing up here. Had he played with other children from these now-abandoned houses? It was hard to imagine sounds of laughter in a place so dismal and heavy with silence. He began to make his way up the driveway towards the house, heart thumping. The front door was boarded up, but he could climb in through a window easily enough.

You can still turn back, said Glum, remaining stubbornly perched on his branch.

It was easy for Glum to say: this house meant nothing to him. But for Caw, it was everything. For so many years his past was a blank – an open sea with no charts to guide him. But this place was a landmark, and he couldn't ignore it any longer. Who knew what he might find inside?

He reached into his jacket pocket and pulled out the crumpled photo – a picture of his parents, from happier times. Crumb had given it to him. The pigeon feral hadn't wanted Caw to come tonight either – grumbling that it was "a waste of time". Caw let his thumb brush across his parents' faces. They looked almost exactly the same as they had when he found them in the Land of the Dead. He'd only managed to share a few precious moments with them, and it had left his heart aching for more. Where better to find out about them than this place?

He owed it to them not to turn back.

As Caw laid a hand on one of the boards over the door, he found that it was loose. He gripped the edge firmly and easily yanked it free, rusting nails and all.

The others posed no more bother, and soon he'd cleared the way.

Caw sensed the crows behind him and turned. Sure enough, all three were perched on the ground.

"Let me go in alone," he said.

Shimmer nodded and Screech hopped back a few steps. Glum looked away with a dramatic toss of his head.

There was a light switch inside, but Caw wasn't surprised that nothing happened when he pressed it. The air was cool and musty. In the gloom, he made out overturned furniture and pictures hanging lopsidedly from the walls. A grand staircase rose from the entrance hall up to a landing, then doubled back on itself to the first floor level. Caw thought he saw something move up there – a rat, or a bird, perhaps, but when he looked again there was nothing.

Caw felt a dim sense of belonging. Small things looked familiar – a lampshade, a doorknob, a tattered curtain. Or maybe it was just his mind playing tricks, wanting to see something significant among the debris of abandoned lives.

Through an archway, Caw could see a sagging couch and wires protruding from a wall socket, and as he walked towards it the view opened on to a dining table.

A rush of fear turned his feet to lead. He knew this room from his nightmares. It was here that it had happened – beside that very table his parents had been murdered by the spiders of the Spinning Man. The table was covered in dust now, but Caw couldn't bring himself to step any closer.

Instead, he turned back to the stairs. They creaked as he climbed. With each step, a haunting nostalgia swelled in his stomach. When he reached the first floor, his feet carried him automatically towards a door with a small placard in the shape of a train. Painted on it were words he recognised from Crumb's lessons – "Jack's Room".

Jack Carmichael.

That had been his name, once.

Caw took a deep breath and pushed the door open.

On the opposite wall, his eyes fell on the window and his knees turned to water. The memories, so dream-like, crystallised into a feeling of pure fear. Caw gripped the doorframe to steady himself.

He remembered the firm hands of his parents as they dragged him from his bed and hauled him towards the window. Their fingers had been so tight it had hurt and their ears had seemed deaf to his screams of panic. Then his father had opened the window and his mother had thrust him out. Caw had watched the ground spinning towards him, felt the terror rising as he fell...

He took a deep breath as the power of the memory faded.

For years, that had been his only remembrance of

them, festering in his mind. Their heartless abandonment. Now he knew it wasn't the full story. It was just one line in a tale that had begun centuries ago – a tale of ferals at war with one another. His parents hadn't been trying to kill him – they'd been *protecting* him, by getting him as far away from the Spinning Man as possible.

Caw opened his eyes, looking away from the window. He was trembling.

The rest of the room was practically empty. A couple of shelves held scraps of paper; and bundles of old clothing had been pushed into one corner. Caw hadn't been expecting the room to be preserved like a museum, but still he felt a rush of rage. Someone had taken all of his things.

The anger seeped away as quickly as it had come, leaving only a numb sorrow. Of course the house had been ransacked and looted. Plenty of petty criminals had taken advantage of the chaos caused by the Dark Summer. Caw guessed a nice house like this would have made for easy pickings.

He let his feet carry him across the mould-covered carpet towards the window. The glass was cracked, and he rubbed a sheen of condensation away with the cuff of his leather jacket. Outside the night was still, the stars bright in a cloudless sky, the moon glowing softly.

Caw sighed. Crumb was right – there was no point in coming here. The past was dead.

Then, in the trees below, he saw something. A pale face materialising from the darkness beside a tree trunk.

Caw's heart jolted. The face didn't move at all, just stared up at him. It was an old man, with skin so white he might have been wearing make-up like a clown. Who was he? And what was he doing here, in Caw's garden?

Caw gripped the window frame. He tried to yank it up to call out to the man, but it didn't budge. He heaved again and it gave a grating screech. He was about to open his mouth when he heard a panicked intake of breath at his back.

"Who are you?" said a voice.

Caw spun round and saw the pile of clothes in the corner stirring. There was a girl lying there, wrapped in a sleeping bag. She was skinny, with dark tangled hair framing her grubby face. She looked a year or two older than him.

Caw stepped back until he collided with the window. His leg muscles wanted to run, but fear paralysed him. He found his voice.

"I..." he started. But what was he supposed to say? Where to start? Her eyes were defiant, but scared too, he noticed, his fear dipping slightly. He raised his hands to show he wasn't a threat. "This is my house," he said. "Who are *you*?"

The girl stood up, shaking the sleeping bag off. She

picked up a baseball bat from beside her, knuckles white as they clenched it.

"Are you on your own?" said the girl.

Caw remembered the man outside and took a quick glance back. But the face by the tree had gone. The crows were nowhere to be seen either.

"Er... yes," he said.

"So, if this is your house, why don't you live here?" the girl said, jabbing the bat at him. She looked like she wouldn't have a problem using it.

Caw kept his distance. "I haven't lived here for a long time," he said. He searched for a better explanation but couldn't think what to say.

The girl hefted the bat again. She looked ready to pounce if he said the wrong thing.

"My parents... they threw me out," he added. It was sort of true.

The girl seemed to relax at that. She lowered the bat a little. "Join the club," she said.

"What club?" said Caw.

The girl frowned. "It's an expression," she said. "It means we're in the same boat."

Caw was getting confused. "This is a house, not a boat," he said.

He wasn't sure why, but the girl laughed at that. "What planet are you from?" she said, shaking her head.

"This one," said Caw. She was making fun of him, he

realised. But at least that was better than trying to bludgeon him with a bat. "Are you on your own?" he asked.

The girl nodded. "I suppose technically I ran away. I've been here a few weeks. My name's Selina, by the way."

"Caw," said Caw.

"That short for something?"

"Not really," he replied.

"I knew there were some empty houses round here," said Selina. She waved the bat, pointing around the room. "This seemed the best of a bad lot."

"Thanks," said Caw. "This used to be my bedroom."

The girl grinned. "It's really nice. The rat droppings make it kind of homely."

Caw couldn't help laughing. It had taken him a while, but gradually, with Pip and Crumb's help, he was getting the hang of talking to people. "It's the charred curtains that make it for me."

Selina leant the baseball bat against the wall. "Look, I can go if you want."

Caw went quiet. He felt sort of strange in the pit of his stomach. No one ever asked what he wanted, so he had no idea. He looked at her ragged clothes and thin face. If he kicked her out, where would she go? He supposed there were other houses she could squat in. But he'd only just met her, and she seemed OK, apart from the baseball bat.

The girl began to gather the sleeping bag up from the floor.

"There's no need to leave," he said quickly. "I'm not staying. I'm finished here."

She paused. "Oh – you live somewhere else now?" she said.

Caw caught a flash of desperation in her eyes. He thought about the Church of St Francis, where he lived with Crumb and Pip. He broke eye contact.

"Sort of," he said.

Selina gave a wry smile. "It's OK – I get it. I can look after myself."

Caw searched her face and wondered if she was just pretending to be tough. He had a mattress at the church, warmth and food. A million times better than here. Could he take her there? There was plenty of room. His heart urged him to say something, but his head argued the other way. He knew Crumb wouldn't like it if he showed up with a stranger. Plus, how could they keep their feral powers a secret from her?

No, it was too risky.

"It's not that," he said. "It's not my place, that's all."

She nodded. "Don't worry about it."

He felt bad. It must get really cold here at night. And how did she eat without any crows to help her?

"Listen," he said, "you look hungry. I could come back, bring you some food if you like."

The girl blushed, but lifted her chin. "I don't need your help," she said.

"No, of course not," said Caw. "I was just... I know places to get food, that's all. In the city."

"So do I," she said defensively. "I'm not going hungry, all right?"

An uncomfortable silence fell over the room. He hadn't meant to offend her.

"Tell you what," she said at last. "How about we share our knowledge? I'll show you where I go, and you can do the same. Two runaways helping each other out?"

Caw blinked. He hadn't been expecting that sort of offer. "What – like, together?"

"Why not?" said Selina. "How about tomorrow night? Ten o'clock."

Caw found himself nodding without even thinking about it.

Screech's soft warble sounded from outside. *They must be worried about me.* Caw didn't want them coming in and scaring Selina.

"I've got to go," he said.

She was watching him closely, her brow wrinkled. "OK," she said. "Bye, Caw – see you tomorrow. I'll guard your parents' valuables till then."

"Valuables?" said Caw. Had she found something in the house?

She smiled again. "Joking," she said.

"Oh, yes," he said, going red. "I get it. Bye then."

He left the room, skin still burning furiously. But as he began descending the stairs, his chest felt light. It had been so long since he'd spoken to a normal person, and apart from a few slips, it hadn't gone too badly. He wondered if he should tell Crumb about the girl. The pigeon feral didn't have a lot of time for non-ferals.

He paused in the living room. All sorts of questions occurred to him now. Where had she run from, and why? How long had she been here and how had she survived? Well, there'd be plenty of time to ask her later.

Find anything? said Shimmer, hopping aside as he closed the front door behind him.

"Not really," Caw lied. "Come on, let's go home."

Nothing at all? said Shimmer, cocking her head.

"It's a ruin," said Caw. "I should have listened to Glum."

Told you so, said Glum.

Caw knew he should tell them about Selina, but they'd only object, just as they had with Lydia. Besides, all his life the crows had kept secrets from him. It was oddly satisfying to have one of his own – even if it was only something small.

They had just reached the end of the front lawn, when a figure stepped out ahead of them.

Caw was gripped with an icy panic. He gasped, and the crows took to the air with wild cries. He backed up, tripped and fell on to his backside. Every fibre of his muscles wanted to run, but he felt completely unable to move.

The man thrust his head forward. "Jack Carmichael?" he said. His voice was soft but urgent. Caw noticed with a wave of revulsion that the man's teeth were sharp shards of enamel jutting from his gums.

You know him? said Screech.

Caw managed to shake his head. It was the man with the white face that he'd seen from his bedroom window. Up close, Caw saw that his features looked pale too – bloodless lips, a squashed little nose and wide, unblinking eyes staring out from behind small tinted spectacles. His face was skeletally thin, with dark hollows beneath his cheekbones, and he had no hair and no eyebrows at all. He wore a long black coat tightly buttoned up.

Shimmer leapt into a branch above the man and let out a harsh shriek.

"I mean no harm," said the man, casting rapid glances to either side. "That's if you *are* Jack Carmichael? The crow talker."

"Who are you?" said Caw, picking himself up. "Why are you spying on me?"

The pale figure reached into his coat and Caw bristled. He saw Glum spread his wings, ready to swoop down. But what the man drew out wasn't a weapon. It was a stone, about half the size of Caw's fist and polished to a jet-black shine.

"This is from Elizabeth," said the stranger, holding it in front of him. "Elizabeth Carmichael."

Caw felt the words tugging at his heart. "My mother? You knew her?"

"Perhaps," said the man. He hesitated. "I suppose I must have. Once." His mouth twitched into the ghost of a smile that vanished just as quickly. "Closer to her than ever now, of course."

Er... what's that supposed to mean? said Shimmer.

Caw stared at the stone sitting in the man's hand. The harder he looked, the harder it was to focus on its edges. It wasn't completely black at all – in its depths, swirls of colour seemed to shift and blur. Caw drew back and the man stepped after him, thrusting the stone towards him.

"It belongs to you, young man. To the crow feral. Take it. *Take it.*"

It might be a trap, said Screech.

Caw could hear the desperation in the stranger's words, but somehow he felt sure it was the truth. The stone *was* his. He knew it, deep in his soul. He extended a hand and the man dropped the stone into his palm. It was lighter than Caw had expected and oddly warm.

"What is it?" asked Caw.

Instead of replying, the man jerked his pale face upwards and shrank back into the darkness. "I must go," he said. "I want nothing to do with it, crow talker. It is yours to bear alone."

Caw turned and saw a pigeon flap out of a window at the rear of his parents' house. One of Crumb's birds. It flew away like a grey shadow.

He closed his fist around the stone. He was dimly aware of the crows making noises, but he was too focused on the strange feeling of the stone throbbing in his palm. Maybe it was just the pulse of his blood?

When Caw looked up again, the stranger was gone. Screech landed on his shoulder and gave his ear a light nip with his beak.

"Ow!" said Caw. "Why'd you do that?" He slipped the stone into his pocket.

Because you weren't listening, said Screech. *Are you OK?*

Caw nodded slowly. "Let's get back to the church. And... we'll keep this to ourselves, all right?"

Screech chuckled. *Who are we going to tell? It's not as if anyone else understands crow, is it?*

"Good point," said Caw.

Chapter 2

Caw woke to a grey pre-dawn light coming through a hole in the church rafters. He heard a sizzle and a smell filled him with a sudden pang of hunger.

Sausages...

He rolled over, scattering the pile of books stacked beside his mattress. At once, the memory of the night rushed back. The stone, the stranger.

Crumb was a few metres away, leaning over his brazier, with his back to Caw, turning spitting sausages in a skillet. Pip sat beside him, letting a mouse run up and down, under and over his sleeve. He was wrapped in an army jacket at least three sizes too big for him and his scruffy fair hair needed a good brush. He looked longingly at the pan.

"They *must* be ready by now!" said the mouse feral.

"Patience," said Crumb.

On one of the roof beams, a pigeon cooed.

"Awake, is he?" said Crumb. "I'm surprised after all that sneaking around last night."

Caw realised that Crumb was talking about him, and blushed, remembering the pigeon from the night before. What exactly had it seen? He sat up and his three trusted crows fluttered down from a window arch, landing at his side. He felt annoyed with himself, first for not being more careful in covering his tracks, but second for being embarrassed. He'd done nothing wrong.

"I had to look," he said. "What's wrong with trying to learn about my past?"

"And did you find anything?" said Crumb, finally turning to him. He was wearing a red cap marked with a tiger's face – the mascot of Blackstone's baseball team – and his long hair poked out on either side. His beard and moustache grew in wispy patches. Caw remembered the first time they'd met in an alleyway. He'd assumed Crumb was just another homeless vagrant living on the streets of Blackstone. But since then, Crumb had become like an older brother to him.

"No," said Caw. His hand went automatically to his pocket, where the dark stone lay, but he disguised the movement by fiddling with his zipper.

"You're lying," said Crumb. "Bobbin said there was someone else in the house."

What's he talking about? said Glum.

"A young lady, he said. He got in through a window to see what you were up to. Isn't that right, Bobbin?"

The fat pigeon on the rafter twitched its head, and Caw remembered thinking he'd seen something up on the landing as he entered the house. It must have been Crumb's bird, watching him.

"It was just a girl," said Caw, sulkily. "Sleeping rough. You don't have to spy on me."

"And you don't have to lie to me," said Crumb. His face looked suddenly older than his twenty-something years. He laid sausages, dripping with fat, into three bread rolls. "We're supposed to be your family, Caw."

You gonna tell him about the weirdo outside? said Shimmer.

Caw shook his head as Crumb offered him a roll on a plate. It didn't sound like Bobbin had seen the pale man, so there was no reason to tell Crumb. It would only lead to more questions about the encounter, and Caw remembered very clearly what the "weirdo" had said – the stone was his to bear alone. Until he knew what it was, it would stay that way.

"Well?" said Pip, through a mouthful. "What girl?"

"Her name is Selina," Caw said. "She's a runaway."

Crumb nodded, biting into his own sandwich and chewing thoughtfully. "You should stay clear of her. No good comes from mixing with humans."

Caw felt an itch of irritation. Crumb couldn't tell

him what to do. Just because he was a few years older. "But—"

"Caw, you have responsibilities now," said Crumb. "As a feral. You can't let people know what you are. Humans can't be trusted."

Caw wasn't so sure. Crumb thought everyone was out to get him. Besides, Caw's friend Lydia was a normal girl. True, he hadn't seen her in the two months or so he'd been living with Crumb. But that wasn't because he didn't want to. It was because he knew her mother didn't want him hanging around with her. Her father Mr Strickham didn't even know about the ferals. They had their own life. A normal one.

"You going to eat that?" said Pip hopefully, pointing at Caw's roll. His own plate was already empty and a couple of mice were polishing off the crumbs.

"Yes," said Caw, drawing the plate closer to his chest.

"You'd better," said Crumb. "We've got training this morning, remember? Then your reading lesson."

Caw groaned. He enjoyed the reading bit, but Crumb insisted on training with their animals three times a week, and that tended to be a lot more painful.

"Do we have to?"

Crumb rolled his eyes. "How many times, Caw? The Spinning Man might be gone, but we don't know how many of his followers are still on the loose, waiting to strike."

An image flashed through Caw's mind – the white spider he had seen scuttling through the graveyard after he had destroyed the Spinning Man. But he'd only seen it for half a second – surely it was his tired mind conjuring up phantoms. He shook off the thought.

"Without a leader—" Caw began.

"There will always be a new enemy," Crumb interrupted sternly.

Before Caw could protest more, a pigeon flashed past, snatched the sandwich from his plate and fluttered above, just out of reach.

"Very funny," said Caw, rolling his eyes. The pigeon dropped the sandwich and Caw caught it. "I'll train twice as hard tomorrow. How about that?"

Crumb gave him a hard stare and Caw couldn't help but look away, embarrassed. After all Crumb had done for him, maybe he did owe the pigeon feral more respect. But a part of him bristled still. Crumb was always telling him what to do. He'd only given Caw a watch so that he could make him show up for meals on time. Surely Caw didn't have to tell him *everything.* "I can't force you," said Crumb. "But remember, this afternoon is Emily's funeral."

"Of course," said Caw. He'd only met the elderly centipede feral once. She'd been a sad old lady, haunted by the deaths of her children in the Dark Summer. "Is it true she has no heir?" he asked quietly.

Crumb nodded. "With her passing, the centipede line will end forever."

A silence fell. Feral powers passed from parent to child. There was no other way.

So, if we're not training, what are we doing? said Shimmer. She was eyeing up his sandwich too, Caw noticed. He tore off a piece and tossed it to her.

"We're going out," he said.

"Can I come too?" said Pip, jumping to his feet.

Caw managed to disguise his grimace as a smile. Sometimes it was fun having Pip around, but other times he followed like a shadow, making Caw feel desperate to be on his own.

"Why don't you stay and train with Crumb?" Caw said. "You'd just be bored with me. Crows are really dull, you know."

Charming, croaked Screech.

Pip looked disappointed, but nodded.

Caw unrolled the blanket he used as a pillow and took out a slim, dark blade – the Crow's Beak. He slid it inside the scabbard he'd made from old leather and slung its straps over his shoulders. Crumb's eyes widened with curiosity. "Expecting trouble?"

Caw shook his head. "Like you said. You never know who's out there." He headed for the stairs and his crows followed.

Boring, are we? said Glum.

Caw waited until they were out of earshot, then whispered, "I didn't want any eyes on us today. Not where I'm planning to go."

Ooh... a secret mission! said Shimmer.

"Just keep a lookout for pigeons," said Caw. "I'll explain on the way."

Blackstone was a city with a lot of history. Crumb had told Caw all about it over several nights – how it had begun hundreds of years before as a settlement by a swampy river, how it had grown when the river was dammed and diverted to irrigate fields for crops. How it had become an important staging post at the crossing of two large trade routes. In the sixteenth and seventeenth centuries, buildings of wood had been razed for those of brick. The city had prospered through the industrial revolution that swept across the country. The river had been widened and rerouted further, with bridges spanning its course.

With each generation, new waves of people came and settled, bringing their cultures and ideas. Steelworks and factories had been replaced by the world of finance and technology. The population boomed and spread. Blackstone had seemed to be on an unstoppable trajectory of progress.

Until the Dark Summer, when the feral war had ripped the city apart.

Eight years had passed since then, but Blackstone

had not recovered. It was like a wounded animal – unable to climb to its feet, but clinging to life.

Caw saw the city differently from the normal people – the ones who stayed on the ground, navigating by street names and landmarks. He knew the sections that were quiet and calm, and the ones that were always crowded. Places of safety and danger. Areas where he could scavenge or where the pickings were meagre. Where he could pass unseen through darkness or where security lights might reveal him. He measured distance not in miles, but in time. Ten minutes to cross from the abandoned train station, via the disused tracks, to the cathedral. Twelve if he took the detour over the rooftops of the old rubber factory.

Everywhere he went, the layers of the past revealed themselves. A church here and there, or old pilings jutting like rotten tooth stumps from the river's shallows where a jetty had once been. And of course the sewers, threading their way in arched tunnels across almost all the city, emptying into pumping stations and sewage works, and ultimately into the far reaches of the River Blackwater.

In his early days of exploring, Caw had never gone down there. But as time wore on, and he grew in confidence, he had begun to venture underground. In the daytime, when the rooftops weren't safe because of construction workers, or police helicopters, the subterranean tunnels offered another way of getting around the city unseen.

But the crows were never keen.

Birds don't like ceilings, said Glum, as they descended through a shaft into a tunnel near the church.

The sky means safety, said Shimmer.

Don't worry, I'll look after you, said Screech, but his voice trembled slightly.

Glum gave a throaty chuckle. *Please, someone pass me the sick bag.*

"We have to make sure we aren't being followed," said Caw. "It's the only way."

He jumped from the bottom of the steel ladder and landed in the tunnel. It was dry, thankfully, but the air was stale and stuffy.

As Caw began to walk along the tunnel; he took a torch from his pocket and flicked it on. The birds swooped ahead at intervals. He'd never met anything down here apart from the odd rat, but still the place made his skin tingle. He wouldn't have wanted to come below on his own.

His back itched and he adjusted the shoulder straps looped under his clothing to make the Crow's Beak sit more comfortably. The ancient weapon wasn't much to look at. A narrow double-edged blade about two feet long and not terribly sharp, but at least it might scare off an attacker long enough for Caw to escape. Besides, it was the sword of the crow line, with the power to open a gateway to the Land of the Dead. It was Caw's duty to bear it.

With his free hand, Caw felt the stone in his pocket. Did that have something to do with the crow line too? It didn't feel particularly remarkable today, but there had to be something special about it, else why would his mother have wanted him to have it? She'd been the crow feral before him, after all.

Had the strange, hairless figure from last night even been telling the truth about knowing Caw's mother? Caw guessed he must have been a feral himself, though he hadn't seen any animals.

Too many questions, and Caw knew only one place he might find answers.

Hello? Earth calling Caw... said Screech.

"What?" said Caw.

You're acting really weird, said Screech. *Glum's talking to you.*

"Sorry," said Caw. "Just thinking about something. What were you saying Glum?"

I said, we're heading west, aren't we? said Glum. The crow's eyes flashed silver in the torchlight. *Are we going back to see that girl?*

"No," said Caw, not breaking his stride. "We're going to Gort House."

Quaker's place! said Glum. *Why d'you want to mix with that old coward?*

"He might know something about this black stone," said Caw. After all, he couldn't just carry it around without the slightest clue as to why it was so special. His mother would want him to find out what it was – she must have left it for him for a reason. He was sure of it.

They trudged on in darkness, through the endlessly winding network of tunnels. They seemed to have been built by a madman. Shafts, wide and narrow, intercepted at different levels in a convoluted maze. Caw walked for twenty minutes, navigating from memory, before climbing several ladders. His feet clanged and echoed through the tunnels as he set out at the higher level.

You sure you know where you're going? said Shimmer, standing on a jutting pipe. *I don't want to get lost down here.*

We know these tunnels like the back of our wings, said Screech, nudging close to her. *I'm cold. Are you?*

Shimmer edged away. *I'm perfectly fine, thank you.*

The tunnel began to climb slightly. Caw counted the vertical shafts as they passed them, until he was sure he'd reached the correct one.

"Our stop," he said.

Leading the way, he prised open the manhole cover from below and peered out. Just as he suspected, he was on a deserted tree-lined road that snaked upwards – the road at the bottom of Herrick Hill that led up to Gort House.

Thank goodness for fresh air! said Shimmer, fluttering up into the branches of a tree. The others rose after her.

Caw clambered out and closed the cover. Gort House was just a short walk up the hill, but he set off at a jog along the side of the road. It was a quiet area and they were unlikely to bump into anyone. Still, he was ready to hide in the bushes if need be.

Even if Quaker was a coward, Caw could trust him. After all, it was the cat feral who had first told him about the Crow's Beak, about his parents, and many other things besides. He was an academic of sorts, specialising in the history and culture of the feral lines. Gort House was stuffed with treasures and artefacts and books – a museum to feralhood.

But as they approached the house, Caw's heart quickened.

Something was wrong.

The gates were open and in the circular driveway was a police car, warning lights spinning silently. Caw held up a hand to stop the crows, but they didn't need telling. They'd already arranged themselves on the railings.

What's going on? asked Screech.

Caw's unease was growing by the second. Had something happened to Quaker? What if a burglar had broken in? Or someone worse than a burglar... He edged inside the gates, along the sculpted shrubbery that lined the front lawn.

"Get your hands off me!" came a cry, followed by the screech of cats.

Caw ducked out of sight, just in time to see Quaker himself shoved out through the front door of his house, arms held behind his back by two policemen. He was impeccably dressed in a brownish tweed suit and red waistcoat, with mustard-coloured moccasins on his feet. A couple of tabby cats tangled around his legs as the cops slammed him against the side of their car. His monocle popped out and one of the policemen crushed it beneath his boot.

"I've done nothing wrong!" said Quaker. "At least tell me what you want."

A grey cat hopped on to the bonnet of the car, hackles rising across its arched spine.

"No, Freddie!" said Quaker.

One of the policemen unbelted his nightstick and swung savagely at the cat, sending it leaping to the ground. It sprinted off into the garden.

"This isn't right," muttered Caw, beginning to step out.

No! said Glum, and Caw hesitated.

"I demand to know what's going on!" said Quaker as a third policeman came out of the house.

"Find anything?" said the cop who'd tried to hit the cat.

"Just a load of old books and dodgy antiques," said the third cop. "We need more men if we're going to do a thorough search."

"Not without a warrant, you won't!" said Quaker.

Smack! The policeman backhanded Quaker across the jaw. "Shut your mouth!"

Caw flinched. He didn't know much about the police, but he knew they weren't supposed to behave like this.

Quaker had gone limp in their grip as he was shoved into the car.

"I can't let them take him," said Caw, but his feet refused to move.

What are you going to do? said Screech. *There are three of them. And you can't show them you're a feral, remember?*

The cops all climbed in after Quaker. The engine revved and the car skidded out of the driveway. Caw pressed himself against the hedge and watched them go with his heart pounding. Several more cats ran from the house, mewling plaintively. They amassed at the gates as the car drove down the hill.

They're police, Caw, said Glum. *Crumb wouldn't want you to get involved, and yet again, I agree with him... Hey!*

Caw had begun to run down the hill, holding on tight to the stone in his pocket, in case it fell out. He knew what he had to do. If he turned into a crow, he could follow from the air. Summoning all his energy, he leapt off the ground, willing the transformation to happen, letting his inner crow take over...

... and landed hard on the road, the wind knocked out of him.

Well, that was embarrassing, said Screech, landing at his side.

Maybe you should be training with Crumb after all, said Glum.

Caw sat up, rubbing his back. Why hadn't it worked? He'd done it before.

"Take me after the police car!" he said to his crows.

He closed his eyes, clenched his fists, and felt the power surge. He might not be able to change into a crow, but he could do the next best thing.

When he opened his eyes again, he saw them coming. Black specks amassing from every direction. The crows of Blackstone were obeying their master.

One by one they descended in a dark swirl, alighting across his clothes. As each fluttering bird attached itself, Caw felt his body lightening, until his feet left the ground completely.

"Follow them!" he said.

Caw's legs wheeled as the crows carried him up, high into the air, swooping along the road's path below. Panic turned to exaltation as Caw gave himself to the power of their wings and the ground shrank away. In the distance, he could see the city's sprawl. He had to stop the car before it reached the crowded metropolis, if he was to avoid being seen by non-ferals. He steered the crows with his mind. There! The car was just ahead, driving slowly along the winding road. The crows speeded up, until Caw was dangling just ten feet above the vehicle. Could he do this? He'd need to time it perfectly.

"Drop me!" he said.

Do what? squawked Screech.

"Now!" shouted Caw.

The talons released him as one and Caw fell, smashing feet first on to the bonnet of the car. He lost his footing and slammed into the windshield. The brakes screeched and the car swerved, and he bounced up over the roof. The world lost all its bearings and Caw braced himself with his arms over his head, until he thumped, side-first, into something very hard.

Caw rolled over, finding himself in the middle of the road. He sat up just in time to see the police car mount the kerb and skid into a tree with a grinding crunch.

Pain shot through Caw's ankle as he stood, but he thought it was just twisted. As that faded, a dozen other injuries screamed for attention. His jacket was torn too. The crows were already coating the trees on either side of the road. Wincing, Caw hobbled towards the police car, dread building in his stomach. *What have I done?* It was spilling smoke from its crumpled bonnet as he yanked open the back door.

The police officers were moving weakly in the front seats. Alive, thank goodness, but still dangerous. Caw leant over Quaker's body and unclipped his safety belt.

"Caw?" said Quaker. He was blinking rapidly, as though in shock.

"Come with me!" Caw said.

"How did you –"

Caw grabbed Quaker's arm and hauled him out. "This way!" he said, leading the way up a grassy verge. Each step sent a fresh spike of pain up his leg. "Off the road."

Quaker stumbled at his side through the undergrowth of the forest. Caw didn't know where he was going, other than as far away from the police as possible. They slid down a leafy slope, tripping over roots and stumps, then splashed across a small stream. Scrambling up the slope on the other side, they reached a small sunken dell. Quaker fell to the ground, panting. Caw's ankle was burning with pain as the crows settled around them.

"Keep a lookout," Caw told them.

"Oh, Caw, what have you done?" sighed Quaker.

A thanks would be nice, said Shimmer.

"What do you mean?" Caw asked the cat feral. "I rescued you."

Quaker's head twitched left and right, as if he'd heard a sound. He staggered to his feet, his eyes were filled with terror. "No, you haven't," he said. "She's watching us, even now."

Caw frowned. "Who's watching us? There's no one here!"

Quaker shook his head, breathing heavily. "You don't understand, Caw."

In the distance, Caw heard shouting. The police. It wouldn't be long before more arrived. "Listen, I need your help," said Caw. "I have something to show you."

He scooped the stone out of his pocket.

Quaker's fidgeting ceased at once. His eyes fixed on the object in Caw's palm.

"No," he said, shaking his head rapidly. "Oh no no no."

Quaker backed away, as though he was afraid the stone might hurt him.

"Come back," said Caw. "What's wrong?"

"That's what she *wants*," mumbled Quaker, never taking his eyes from the stone. "It all makes sense. How did you get it?"

"Someone gave it to me," said Caw. "He said it came from my mother."

Quaker reached the lip of the dell. "That may be so. But it's not safe, Caw. *You're* not safe. Put it away, for God's sake."

Caw tucked the stone back into his pocket. "Why? What is it?"

Quaker's throat bobbed. "Get rid of it," he said. "Tell no one you have it. Not Crumb, not Lydia, not Velma – no one! Your mother would have told you the same. It is the crow feral's burden. Take it somewhere where no one can ever find it again, and please… I beg you… keep it away from me."

He turned and ran, darting away between the trees.

"Wait!" said Caw. "I need your help!"

But Quaker was gone.

There's no pleasing some people, said Shimmer. Her voice seemed distant and muffled. Caw shook his head. Perhaps he'd fallen harder than he thought on the road.

"I've found footprints!" shouted one of the police.

A bird squawked from a distance, and Caw saw it was Glum, perched on a branch twenty feet away. "What did you say?" said Caw.

This way! said Glum. *I'll get us out of here.*

Caw ran after him, ankle throbbing. With every step, he could feel the stone bouncing against his side.

Chapter 3

As Caw rushed up to the graveyard followed by his crows, he saw Crumb and Pip waiting at the gates. A stranger might have thought they were two very mismatched brothers, one over six foot tall and the other barely four and a half.

They've made a bit of an effort, haven't they? said Glum.

Crumb had combed his hair and shaved. He was wearing his best pair of shoes – or perhaps he'd just put new tape around the old ones. Pip wore a crumpled black dinner suit, the jacket baggy over his shoulders, and he'd even found a bow tie from somewhere. Caw suddenly felt self-conscious about his own torn coat and scruffy boots.

The pigeon feral grunted. "So you decided to show up at last. Where've you been all day?"

"Sorry," said Caw. "I lost track of time."

"Hmm," said Crumb. "Come on, the service is about to start."

Caw trudged along the path after Crumb and Pip, while his crows flapped up and landed above the chapel door. His ankle still ached a little, but he was hardly limping now.

Like the ruined Church of St Francis, this place was long abandoned and the graveyard mostly untended. It felt strange being back here – the place where his own parents were buried. Crumb led them around the other side of the church where Caw saw a small gathering of people around a freshly dug grave. A mound of soil stood at the graveside waiting to be piled into the hole in the ground.

There were about a dozen people present besides Crumb, himself and Pip. Caw recognised a few of the other ferals. There was Ali, dressed in a slim-fitting black suit and still clutching his briefcase, which buzzed softly with the swarm of bees held inside. Racklen, the hulking wolf feral, stood at his side. Caw was disappointed not to see Madeleine, the raven-haired girl in the wheelchair, but he saw two of her squirrels perched in the branches at the edge of the graveyard.

He tried to scan the other faces without staring. There were people of every age. A girl of maybe four or five had a huge Dobermann sitting patiently at her side. An old man was leaning on a stick, though he didn't seem to be accompanied by any creature. Two boys, who looked identical, stood on either side of a large, floppy-eared hare, its nose twitching. At the back stood a youngish couple with a baby in a pram. A hawk sat perched on the pram's rim, and beside it, strangely, was a raccoon. Were both parents ferals?

At the head of the grave stood a figure Caw knew very well indeed. Mrs Strickham was dressed in a long black coat with pale gleaming buttons. She looked more severe than he remembered her from two months ago, the lines of her face taut. She acknowledged Caw with a brief nod and a smile that softened her features. She was holding a white rose. "Please, everyone, gather around," she said.

Caw joined the group, which formed a ring around the empty grave.

No one spoke for several seconds. Caw had never been to a funeral before, let alone a feral one. He wasn't sure what was supposed to happen. Then he noticed that, one by one, the crowd were turning towards the church. He followed their gaze, up the path, and his eyes fell on the strangest thing.

Not the coffin itself – that was a simple casket, made of tightly woven wicker – but the fact that it was *moving*, gliding across the uneven ground as if on a cushion of air. Caw suddenly realised what he was seeing. There were centipedes under the coffin, thousands of them, their tiny legs scurrying along.

"They're carrying her!" he murmured.

"It's their final duty," said Crumb.

When they reached the graveside, the centipedes descended the slope down into the earth, taking the coffin with them. As it came to rest at the bottom, Mrs Strickham cleared her throat.

"Thank you all for coming," she said, speaking over the grave. "Emily would have been honoured to see you here." Several heads bobbed in acknowledgement. Not for the first time, Caw felt a stranger in the company of the ferals and the history they shared.

"I first met Emily fifteen years ago," Velma Strickham continued. "Some of you are too young to remember a time before the Dark Summer, when many of our kind were known to one another." A smile crept over Mrs Strickham's face as she said the words. "Emily ran a ferals group under the guise of a knitting circle, and many struggling with their powers benefited from her kindness and advice. She was a loving mother to her three girls as well. I say this from personal experience, but it is always hard to know when as a feral parent you should tell your children." She paused. "When to burden them with their destiny."

Caw swallowed as a fresh pang of grief rose from his heart. His mother was snatched away before she ever had the chance to speak with him.

His hand stroked the stone in his pocket again and he felt suddenly empty. There was a lot his mother hadn't told him. He looked around the assembled faces. Surely someone here must know about the stone? But could he really trust them? The words of Quaker flashed through his mind.

Tell no one you have it. Not Crumb, not Lydia, not Velma – no one.

Crumb put his arm around Caw's shoulder, as if he sensed his discomfort, and Caw let his fingers release the stone.

"Emily was preparing to tell her children about her powers when the Dark Summer fell upon us," said Mrs Strickham. "You all suffered in those months. We lost many. But few suffered as Emily did."

The air seemed to have become chillier as a light wind picked up, ruffling the treetops and blowing leaves across the graveyard. Caw saw more birds gathered in the branches – thrushes, woodpeckers, and an owl. All seemed to be watching intently. The old man with the stick shifted a little, and a ferret poked its head from the bottom of his trouser leg.

"Mamba's snakes were trying to find Emily herself, but instead they found her daughters," Mrs Strickham said, her voice close to cracking. "Their deaths were quick and that was a small mercy. After that Emily fought on, somehow. Without her, we could never have defeated our enemies during the Dark Summer. But it took all she had and afterwards she was never the same.

"I will not say her twilight years were happy, because we do not need to sugarcoat our existence, and Emily would be contemptuous of such a lie. But nor do I think she died a wretched death. In fact, she told me just a week ago that she was planning to set up her knitting circle once more. That can only mean she had found a sort of peace."

Mrs Strickham paused. Caw searched the faces of the other mourners, and saw that several were in tears.

"With Emily, the centipede line ends," said Mrs Strickham. "Hers is a double death, and our world is poorer for her passing. May she rest in peace."

"Rest in peace," the crowd muttered, and Caw joined in.

Mrs Strickham threw the rose on to the coffin. Racklen stepped forward and began to shovel earth into the grave. The centipedes, Caw noticed, remained in the ground with their mistress.

"You went to see Quaker, didn't you?"

The question startled Caw. He whipped his head around to see Pip, then turned back to keep his eyes on Mrs Strickham.

"You followed me!" he whispered.

"You might have got away from the pigeons, but mice can crawl down drains," said Pip. "We lost track of you when you went up a ladder though."

Caw let out a silent sigh of relief. The last thing he

needed was Crumb finding out about the incident with the police car. He would *definitely* not approve.

The mourners were beginning to drift away now and Crumb had gone over to speak with the ferret feral, greeting him with a hug. Pip's mice were scampering around with the raccoon, climbing its fur while it tried to shake them off. Ali's bees flew lazily around the meadow flowers that lined the graveyard, while their master spoke to the girl with the Dobermann.

"So what did you want with Quaker?" asked Pip. "Don't worry, I haven't told Crumb."

"Do whatever you like," said Caw. "I just wanted to ask him more about my parents."

Pip frowned. But before the mouse feral could ask any more questions, Crumb beckoned them over. "You two, come and say hello to Mr Duddle."

Pip did as he was told without question, but Caw hung back. Why did Crumb have to boss him around all the time? He pretended he hadn't heard, he went over to the wolf feral instead, who was still shovelling, sweat glistening on his forehead.

The huge man paused as Caw came close and buried the shovel in the ground. "Crow talker," he said flatly.

Caw wasn't really sure how to respond. The wolf feral didn't seem about to carry on digging, but didn't say anything either. Caw began to wish he'd gone with Pip.

"I just wanted to ask," Caw said slowly, "about the girl

who talks to squirrels. Is she all right?" Caw remembered Racklen was the one pushing Madeleine's wheelchair that day when he'd first met them.

"Why are you asking me?" rumbled the wolf feral.

Caw shrank back a little. "I... I thought you might be friends," he said.

Something brushed against Caw's leg, and when he looked down he saw that it was a fox. Velma Strickham was standing a few paces behind, staring fiercely at Caw.

"Would you come with me a moment please?" she asked. "There's someone who'd like to say hello." Without waiting, she turned and headed down the path through the graveyard.

"I guess I should go," Caw mumbled at Racklen. "I'm sorry."

The wolf feral's glare softened, and he shook his head. "No, crow talker," he said quietly. "*I* am sorry. Emily was a friend of mine, and today has been hard. Madeleine has a hospital appointment today, but she is doing well."

Caw nodded.

"And by the way," said Racklen, "all ferals owe you their thanks. What you did in the Land of the Dead... it was very brave."

He thrust out a huge, soil-stained paw of a hand. Caw took it, blushing, then ran down the hill after Mrs Strickham. She had already reached her car and opened the door.

Lydia stepped out. Her mass of red hair was loose over her shoulders and her fringe came right to her eyeline, making her delicate face seem even smaller than normal. She was wearing jeans and a long-sleeved T-shirt with a picture of a seal reclining on an iceberg. He studied the words for a moment. It read "Just Chill". He looked up to see that his friend was beaming at him.

Caw rushed up to her, grinning, then wasn't sure exactly what to do. She opened her arms and Caw realised she wanted to give him a hug. He leant forward and let her do it, wrapping his arms awkwardly around her. She squeezed him tightly.

"I haven't seen you for ages," Lydia said.

Caw shot a glance at Mrs Strickham. Her attention was on the churchyard, but he sensed she was listening to everything he said.

"No," Caw replied. "I've been... erm... busy."

"Still living at the church?"

Caw nodded. "What's been happening with you?"

Lydia blew out her cheeks. "A lot, I guess." She looked across, waiting until her mother had climbed into the car and closed the door. She lowered her voice. "Caw, it's been terrible! Mum hardly lets me out of the house. I think she's worried I'll get into trouble. And Dad's lost his job."

"Oh no! Why?" said Caw.

Lydia shrugged. "Supposedly because of the escaped convicts," said Lydia. "But Dad says it's political. Something to do with a new Police Commissioner wanting to replace the governor at the prison. We might have to move out of the house. But anyway..." she punched his arm. "You've been so busy you couldn't come and see me?"

Caw could tell she was upset. "We need to get going," said Lydia's mother impatiently, hand on the car roof.

"Crumb's been training me really hard," said Caw, and he knew at once how lame it sounded. He rolled up his sleeve and showed her his bruises from where Crumb's pigeons had shoved him over a park bench two days before. There were several others too from the fall off the police car – grazes and a deep purple welt across his wrist.

"Ouch!" she said. "Did you do something to upset him?"

"It's worse than it looks," Caw said guiltily. "He's been teaching me to read too. There's still lots of words I don't know, but I'm getting there."

"That's great!" said Lydia, though a cloud passed across her face as she spoke. "And how are Screech and Glum?"

"The same," said Caw. "Well, not quite. I've got a new one called Shimmer. She's cool. Screech really likes her."

Lydia giggled. "You mean he has a crush."

I do not! croaked a voice from above. Caw saw Screech was perched on the branch of an elm tree. *I just admire her flying ability.*

The car's engine started up. Mrs Strickham had climbed in and shut the door.

"We went to my old house yesterday," said Caw. "And guess what – we found a girl living there!"

"Oh?" said Lydia, with a small grimace. "What, like squatting?"

"I guess so," said Caw. "Her name's Selina. She's homeless, like I was. I'm going to teach her to scavenge."

"That's... that's cool, Caw," said Lydia. "Maybe I can come too?"

Caw hadn't been expecting that. "Why would you want to scavenge? You've got proper food, y'know – on a *plate*."

"Because it's fun," said Lydia. "When are you heading out?"

"Er... I don't know," said Caw. "Look, Lydia, maybe it's best if you don't. It might not be safe."

She frowned. "I can look after myself."

"Last time you got mixed up with me, I almost got you killed," said Caw.

The stone weighed heavy in his pocket. The dangers of the past might be behind him, but new ones lingered in waiting, he was sure. Until he knew what the stone was, and why Quaker was so scared of it, he couldn't risk letting Lydia get close again.

The car window opened, and Mrs Strickham's face appeared. "We need to go now, Lydia. Your father will get suspicious if we're out shopping much longer."

"I'm sorry," said Caw. "I just don't want to get you into trouble."

"Come on, sweetheart," said her mother.

Lydia bit her bottom lip. "Caw, I thought we were friends," she said.

He blinked at her sudden fierce tone. They'd certainly been through a lot together, but he'd never really had friends, apart from the crows. "We... we are," he said.

She turned away and opened the car door, climbing inside. As she fastened her seatbelt she shook her head sadly. "Then why don't you act like it?"

The door slammed before Caw could answer and the car sped off, leaving him standing alone at the edge of the graveyard.

Chapter 4

Caw was glad he'd told his crows to wait at the end of the street, because Selina was standing outside the house that night when he arrived. The last thing he wanted to do was scare her off by chatting to birds.

She looked taller tonight, maybe even taller than him, but then he realised she was wearing stacked boots, made of leather and laced up to her ankles. The rest of her clothes were black too, with a knee-length skirt over dark tights and a fitted black jacket zipped up to her chin. He wondered what Lydia would have made of her. She had headphones in her ears and took them out as he approached.

"You're late," she said.

Caw pulled out his watch and checked. It was ten past ten. "Sorry," he said. "There were a ton of police patrols about tonight. I had to come the long way."

"You're supposed to put that round your wrist, you know," she said, pointing at the watch. "Anyway, what's wrong with the police? You in trouble or something?"

Caw blushed. "It's not that. I just..." he didn't know how to finish.

"It's fine," she said quickly. "Actually, I wasn't sure you'd come at all." She blew into her hands, which were encased in fingerless gloves.

"I said I would. Ready to go?"

"Sure," she said. "Where d'you take a girl for dinner round here?"

Caw tried not to blush even deeper, but from the heat rising behind his cheeks he knew he had failed miserably. Surely she wasn't expecting a restaurant. "We're just scavenging," he said.

"And I was only joking," she said. "Tell you what, you show me where to find a good meal, and I'll work on your sense of humour radar."

Caw grinned. He knew she was mocking him, but he didn't mind. "Are you hungry?"

"Always," said Selina.

"I know a good Chinese place," said Caw. "They have a really nice table out back by the bins."

Selina frowned.

"That was a joke too," said Caw.

Selina clapped. "Oh, right! You're learning. It sounds divine!"

They set off down the street. Out of habit, Caw stuck to the shadows where he could, but Selina didn't look worried. She moved with a spring in her step, sometimes straying into the middle of the deserted roads or kicking cans along the street. While Caw's head jerked at every sound the city made – a far-off dog barking, the revving of a motorbike engine – Selina didn't even seem to notice them.

They soon reached an area littered with building machinery and cranes. It had been a forgotten construction site for as long as Caw could remember, probably abandoned in the aftermath of the Dark Summer. Caw took off his jacket and laid it over the barbed wire at the top of a fence.

"This is the quickest way into the city centre," he said, hoisting himself to the top. Straddling the fence, he reached down to Selina.

He needn't have bothered. "I'm fine, thanks," she said, ignoring the hand and scampering up. She swung her body over the top, then dropped into a crouch on the other side. "So where did you say you lived again?" she asked.

Caw climbed down as well. "Er... I didn't," he said. "I move around."

Caw didn't want to keep secrets from her – but he still wasn't ready to tell her about the church. And he was grateful that Selina didn't push it. He remembered when he'd first met Lydia, and she'd bombarded him with questions.

"I used to live in a tree-house," he said.

"No way!" she replied. "Where?"

"In the old park, north of here," said Caw.

"That place is *creepy*!" said Selina.

"I kind of liked it." Caw remembered the place fondly now, but in the winter it had sometimes got so cold there was frost on his blanket in the morning. "How are you with heights?" he asked. "The safest way is over the rooftops from here."

Selina swatted an insect off her shoulder, looking up at the buildings ahead. "I'll give it a try," she said.

Caw went first, placing his feet and hands in the cracked mortar and climbing up to a broken first-floor window. This place had been a military barracks, Crumb had told him. Selina made it up easily. Caw was glad he hadn't invited Lydia – she would have slowed them down. They crossed a long room littered with old papers, then climbed two sets of stairs to the roof fire escape. As they came through, the city spread out beyond.

"Oh, wow!" said Selina.

Caw saw the wonder in her face and felt a rush of pride. This was one of his favourite views as well. He set off at a light jog and Selina followed.

"There's a jump coming up," he said. "Not big, but follow my lead."

He reached the edge of the building and launched himself over the two-metre gap. Then he turned to watch Selina, but she had already jumped, landing neatly beside him.

"You're a natural," he said, impressed.

"I take – I *took* – gymnastics at school," she said, "before I ran away. It's cool up here! It's like being a bird, looking down on everything."

Caw instinctively checked the sky, surprised that until then he hadn't thought about his crows at all. He saw Shimmer and Screech sitting on an aerial about twenty metres to his left. Glum would be nearby too. They were keeping their distance.

They continued across the rooftops and Selina didn't put a foot wrong. Gradually they penetrated closer to the heart of the city.

"So, do you miss school?" Caw asked.

"Er... sure," said Selina. "Well, I miss my friends."

"How long have you been away from home?"

He checked her expression to make sure he wasn't being too nosey, but she looked fine.

"A couple of months," she said. "I didn't think I'd be gone this long, really. I just wanted to be on my own for a while at first, but then... well, I found I quite liked it."

Caw paused at the edge of a building, peering into the road below. He came this way because most of the shops were boarded up and the streetlights were never switched on, but there were still cars about, and a few people.

"So how've you got by?" he said. "For food and stuff like that?"

"It's been hard at times," she replied. "I begged a bit in the city, did some things I shouldn't."

"What do you mean?" asked Caw, nervously.

"Oh, nothing too bad," she said. "I learnt how to survive, that's all."

Caw was glad to let the subject drop. "We have to climb down here," he said. "There's a network of alleys that leads to the river – that's where the restaurant is." He pointed to a drainpipe. "You OK with that?"

Selina nodded. She touched his arm. "Wait, Caw – I want to ask you something."

"Yes?"

She paused. "Tell me if it's none of my business, but... you said that house was yours. Where are your parents?"

"Dead," Caw replied. "A long time ago."

"Oh," said Selina. "I'm sorry." Again, she didn't pursue it.

"That's all right," said Caw, shrugging. "What about your folks? Why'd you run away?"

Selina's mouth twisted a little. "My dad walked out before I was born," she said. "Mum and I have never really got along. She's got a really important job. Works ridiculous hours. Probably hasn't even noticed I'm gone." She smiled. Unconvincingly, Caw thought.

"Do you think you'll ever go back?" he asked.

Selina lowered herself over the edge of the building, gripping the drainpipe in both hands.

"I don't know," she said.

She slid down quickly, and Caw followed.

Struggling to keep up? said Shimmer, tip-toeing along the parapet of the building.

"A bit," Caw muttered, as he landed beside Selina.

"D'you always talk to yourself?" she asked.

Caw pasted on a grin. "Sometimes – sorry."

Soon they reached the river, where the giant wharves stood like hulking silhouettes. Caw had never liked the Blackwater. Perhaps it was simply because he couldn't swim, but there was something about the impenetrable darkness of the water too, like a black abyss. Crumb told him it was so dirty that if you drank a single mouthful, you'd die within a day. He said there were stories in the *Blackstone Herald* about people falling in and never being seen again. Caw didn't doubt it. He remembered Miss Wallace giving him a book once about a creature with a woman's body and a fish's tail that lived in the river. The water had looked blue though, rather than black and full of filth. As they walked the deserted path that ran alongside the river, he wondered if there were ferals who could talk to fish.

"You OK?" asked Selina.

Caw nodded. She was at his side, looking at him curiously.

There were boats of various sizes moored up – most looked completely abandoned, like floating carcasses butting up against the dockside. Some had names like *Fair Maiden*, or *The Floating Rose*, which seemed completely at odds with their peeling paint, or the years' worth of weed growing up their battered hulls.

One boat, in better repair than most, was unmarked. It had a slightly sunken cabin positioned in the middle of the craft and through a glass window Caw saw a cabin piled with crates and boxes.

"Maybe we'll find something in there," said Selina, pointing.

Caw looked up and down the bank nervously. He couldn't see anyone – the nearest bridge was some distance away, where cars trailed across like streaks of light.

"I don't know," he said. "Isn't that stealing?"

Selina shrugged. "I guess so. Seriously, have you never taken anything before?"

Caw blushed. "Yes," he said. When he'd been younger and more desperate. Clothes off people's washing lines, bread from an open truck. But this seemed different. He had other ways to survive.

Selina reached into her pocket and took out something glinting on a leather strap. Caw's eyes widened and he felt automatically inside his coat. "My watch! How did you –"

Selina gave a crooked grin. "Up there on the roof, when I touched your arm."

Caw was impressed, and a tiny bit annoyed. "I didn't even feel it," he said.

"Well, that's all I meant when I said I've learnt to survive," she said. "I never took anything off people who'd really suffer." She handed Caw back the watch and he tucked it deep inside his coat pocket.

"Come on," urged Selina. "No one will notice – we won't take much. Plus we don't have to go all the way into the city."

She was right, sort of, thought Caw. But it still didn't feel good. He looked around again and saw the three crows had alighted nearby on another boat's roof. Caw knew they would side with Selina. Crows didn't have a lot of time for the finer points of human morals. He wondered what Lydia would say though.

"There's no one around," said Selina, obviously mistaking his gaze for fear. "It's safe."

She jumped on the boat, and Caw followed her. It rocked slightly under his weight. Selina went to the padlocked cabin door and took something out of her pocket, her tongue held between her teeth in concentration as she worked at the padlock.

"What's that?" he said.

"Swiss army knife," said Selina. "Never leave home without it." With a click, the lock cracked open. She grinned and began to unloop a chain from the door handle. The sound was deafening against the river's silence. "How d'you think I got through your back door?"

"Maybe we shouldn't..." said Caw.

"Chill out," said Selina, heading inside. Caw shot a glance around, just in case, then crept after her. She was already crouched beside one of the boxes, using another of the knife's tools to prise open the lids. She strained for a second, and it popped open. Caw saw stacks of tins inside.

"Urgh! Mushroom soup," said Selina. She moved on to the next. "That's more like it!" she said. "Biscuits!" She stood up and tossed two packets to Caw. He caught them clumsily and put them in his inside pocket. At least they would make the crows happy.

"Hey, look what I found!" said Selina. She was kneeling over a crate containing some sort of round fruit. She tossed one to Caw.

He caught it, and sank his teeth into the flesh. Juice exploded in his mouth.

"Wow!" he said. "What is it?"

Selina snorted through her nose. "You've never had a peach before?"

Caw shook his head, taking another bite. "This is the best thing I've ever—"

A crow's shriek split the air above. Selina jumped, and Caw heard Shimmer from outside. *Danger!* she squawked.

Caw dropped the remains of the peach and grabbed Selina's hand. "Someone's coming," he hissed.

"How do you know that?" whispered Selina.

He was just beginning to creep back towards the cabin door, when he felt the boat shift again beneath his feet. Someone else had climbed on board. He pointed towards the back of the cabin. "Hide!" he said. Selina looked terrified, but did as he said, sneaking out of sight behind a stack of crates.

Caw noticed there was a smaller door to the rear of the cabin. He stabbed a finger towards it and Selina nodded. As Caw peered through the crack in the main door, he saw two figures standing on the prow.

They weren't police – he could see that at once. One was a woman – it was hard to tell how old – wearing ill-fitting patchwork clothes of several textures and styles. She had wild hair sticking up at strange angles and her top teeth peeked out over her lip. The person at her side couldn't have been more different. He was impeccably dressed in a white suit so bright it seemed to glow. He must have been about fifty and his slightly jowly, lined face would have been friendly but for his small, chilly blue eyes. He wore a white cowboy hat.

The woman twitched. "We-we-we know you're in

there!" she stammered in a high-pitched voice. "C-c-come out, little boy."

Caw's breath was building in his lungs, and he tried to let it out slowly. He knew he could probably get away with the help of the crows, but what about Selina? The woman had only said "little boy" – perhaps they didn't even know Selina was inside. He had to cause a distraction so she could escape.

He pushed the door open slowly and stepped out. "Who are you?" he said, trying to sound unafraid.

"Allow us to intro*duce* ourselves," drawled the man in the white suit. He took off his hat, and beneath it his hair was white too and neatly combed.

"My name is Mr Silk, and this esteemed lady goes by the name of Pinkerton."

"What do you want?" said Caw. He looked around for his crows, ready to give the word.

"A few birds aren't going to help you now," said the man.

Caw flinched. If they knew he was the crow talker, that could only mean one thing.

"You're ferals," he said.

The woman with the wild hair began to chuckle, and the deck came alive, shifting in many parts. Hundreds of eyes glinted up at Caw, as a swarm of rats rushed towards him.

Chapter 5

Caw stumbled backwards as they came for him. He kicked out at one of the piled crates, sending it sliding and shattering in the path of the rats. But they just streamed over the top, unrelenting, their furry bodies rustling.

Caw reached out and snatched a wooden pole with a metal hook at the end. He swept it across the deck, scattering as many rats as he could. But soon they were on the pole as well, scurrying along its length. Caw hurled it away. He hopped up on a barrel and on to the top of the cabin, landing in a crouch. He saw that the woman's eyes had rolled back in her head, revealing bloodshot whites that flickered as she controlled the rodents. They attacked the sides of the cabin in waves, piling on top of each other as they scrambled up and fell back, unable to gain purchase with their clicking claws.

"Do you have any comprehension," said the man in

the white suit, "of how quickly these creatures could devour you? A rat will eat until it is incapable even of moving. They aren't picky either – muscle, bone, cartilage – it's *all* the same to them."

Caw looked around for an escape route, but the rats were everywhere. There was only the water, and he couldn't swim. And what about Selina? Had she managed to get away through the other door yet? "Just tell me what you want," he said.

Mr Silk spread his arms. There was something strange about the material of his suit, Caw thought, but he couldn't work out what it was.

"Don't play games with me, boy," said the suited man. "It's the stone we want."

Caw swallowed.

"I don't know what you're talking about," he said.

Mr Silk smiled. "Come, come," he said. "Let's not waste each other's time. Pinkerton?"

The woman twitched a hand and the rats went into a frenzy, piling on top of one another, forming a ramp at the side of the cabin. One managed to scramble up and on to Caw's foot. He kicked it away.

Then, with a thought, he summoned his crows. Their black shapes gathered in his consciousness and he sent them swooping towards Pinkerton.

Screech, Glum and Shimmer dived through the air. At the same moment, Mr Silk's jacket seemed to burst outwards. Hundreds of fluttering creatures peeled off the material and flew up to intercept the crows. Moths...

I can't see! Glum cried out as the winged creatures enveloped him. Screech and Shimmer veered off wildly as they too were cloaked with insects.

"Let's try again, shall we," said Mr Silk. "Give me the Midnight Stone."

'D-d-do it!" cackled Pinkerton. "She wants it. She wants it."

She? thought Caw. Who is *she?*

He felt a stinging pain in his ankle, and cried out. A rat hung by its teeth. Another clambered over his foot and on to his trousers, chattering horribly. The rest followed, swarming up his legs. Caw felt them sink their jaws into his flesh as one and he screamed, thrashing. More rats scrambled over his back. An endless stream. There was only one way out now. He raised himself up – fighting the weight of the squirming bodies clinging all over him – and he leapt off the boat's edge into the freezing water below.

It swallowed him, and for a moment all he could see were bubbles in the blackness. His clothes dragged at his limbs, but then his head broke the surface and he sucked in a breath.

Panic gripped his heart. His head went under again and water choked him. He splashed back to the surface, coughing. There were rats in the river too, their bodies bobbing all around. The bank was only a few feet away, but he couldn't reach it. He sank once more.

This time his feet touched the gravelly bottom of the Blackwater. He pushed off with his toes, lunging, just managing to grab a rope holding the boat against the bank. Sucking in rapid breaths, he heaved his sodden body out of the water.

Mr Silk was already standing on the riverside path. His moths fluttered all around him, then settled as one, forming a seamless camouflage over his jacket. Caw shot a glance at the boat and saw that the cabin's back door was open. At least Selina had got out.

"You cannot escape us," said Mr Silk calmly. "She wants the stone and she will have it."

Caw hesitated. He didn't even know what the stone was, but it had been entrusted to him by his mother. The one thing she'd left him. No way would he hand it over without a fight.

"I don't know what you're talking about," he said. His crows were nowhere to be seen. He looked around for Selina, but he couldn't see her anywhere. Then he felt something digging into his back. Of course! He had another weapon.

Caw threw off his sodden jacket and drew the Crow's Beak from its harness.

Mr Silk looked at the sword calmly as he held out

one arm, chivalrously, to help Pinkerton disembark. The tide of rats followed her.

"Please," he said. "There's no need to be uncivil."

"Get away from him," said another voice.

Caw spun around and saw a small shape coming along the path. His heart plummeted as he realised it was Pip, with a huge swarm of mice at his heels.

"Get out of here!" said Caw. Pip shook his head. With a thrust of his arm, he sent his mice charging past Caw towards the new ferals.

The rats met the mice in a seething battle, bodies tipping over each other with horrible sounds and squeals as the rodents bit one another. Seeing that Mr Silk had disappeared, Caw took his chance and jumped over the scrapping mice and rats, launching himself at Pinkerton. She backed away, flapping her arms, until she tripped and landed on the ground. Caw brought the tip of the Crow's Beak to her neck.

"P-p-please..." she said. "Don't kill me!"

"Call off your rats!" he said.

The nattering teeth and the screeching died down, leaving silence. "Pip?" Caw called out, looking behind him.

Mr Silk had the boy gripped from behind, legs off the ground, with a slender silver blade resting against his throat. How had the moth feral even got there, past Caw? It was a narrow path...

Rats melted away into the shadows, and the mice

gathered around Pip, keeping their distance.

"Let him go," said Caw.

Mr Silk grinned. "Or what? You'll kill her? I'd guess you care a good deal more for this boy than I do for poor Pinkerton there. Run her through, for all I care."

"W-what... b-but..." said Pinkerton, her eyes dancing madly.

"So hand it over before he bleeds," said Mr Silk.

"Don't give him anything!" said Pip.

"Patience is not one of my virtues," said Mr Silk. He pressed the blade hard against Pip's white throat.

Caw let his mind reach out to his crows, summoning them as fast as he could. He sensed their crow spirits flicker in response, but it was Shimmer who shot through the air first. She raked her claws along Mr Silk's hand. He yelled out in pain and dropped his knife, then Glum thumped into his shoulder. A cloud of moths erupted from the feral as he fell to the ground.

The crows wouldn't be able to keep Mr Silk down for long. Caw grabbed Pip and together they ran along the path, then skidded around a corner, entering an alleyway between two wharf buildings.

They ran until Caw's lungs burned, trying to put as much distance between them and the river as possible. Caw's leg was really hurting. As they reached a road bridge, Selina's voice called out from above.

"This way!"

She was peering down from a set of narrow steps leading up the side of the bridge. Caw and Pip sprinted towards her and together they climbed up on to a deserted road. The crows landed safely on the edge of the bridge in a flutter of black wings.

Did you see Shimmer? said Screech. *She got him right between the eyes!*

A few mice scurried along the side of the road, making Selina stare in wonder.

"Who is she?" asked Pip, looking at Selina.

Caw rounded on him, seizing his shoulders.

"Never mind that. Why were you following me?" he said savagely. "You nearly got yourself killed!"

Pip's lower lip began to wobble. "I just wanted to help you."

"I don't need your help!" said Caw. "I want you to stop following me." He looked around, expecting to see pigeons nearby. "Are Crumb's spies here too?"

"What spies? What are you talking about?" asked Selina. She was shaking her head in confusion. "Who were those people? And why were all those rats attacking like that? And the moths? It doesn't make any sense."

"It's hard to explain," said Caw.

"Well, maybe you should try," said Selina. "We nearly got killed. Did you know those people? What did they want?"

Things were moving so fast, Caw couldn't keep up.

But the words of Felix Quaker still rang in his head. Neither Selina nor Pip had heard what Mr Silk said about the stone. The secret was safe. "I don't know," he said. "Look, you should go back to my house."

Selina frowned. "Hang on – what do you mean? Where are you going?"

Back to the church, said Glum. *Quite enough adventures for one evening.*

"And what's with the crows?" snapped Selina. "I swear they've been following us since we left your house."

"Maybe you should just tell her," said Pip. As if on cue, the mice raced up the side of his trousers, disappearing into his clothes.

Caw glared at him.

"Tell me what?" said Selina. "Are you two some sort of circus act?"

"It's nothing," he said. "Please, you'll be safer if you're not with us, that's all."

He broke away from her. He needed time to think.

"No way!" she said, following him. "You can't just run off. Tell me – what is going on?"

Want us to stall her? said Screech, swooping so close over Selina's head she had to duck. She looked up angrily, but kept on after Caw, then stopped and glared at Pip.

"You tell me, then, mouse boy," she said.

Caw took a deep breath and spun round. "OK, I'll explain. But not here." If there were enemy ferals on the loose, Caw could only think of one person who might be able to help. He set off north, away from the river. It was time to visit the most powerful feral in Blackstone.

"Where are we going?" said Pip, trotting to keep up.

"To see Velma Strickham," said Caw.

On the way, Caw began to explain to Selina all about the secret world of the ferals, with Pip interrupting every so often. At first, she struggled to take it in, but Screech and Shimmer seemed happy to demonstrate that he really could communicate with them by landing on each shoulder on command. Glum refused.

I'm not a performing monkey, he grumbled.

Pip had enjoyed showing off, forming a chain of mice across his arms, then making them sit in a perfect circle on the ground.

"That's incredible," said Selina her eyes wide. "I don't remember the Dark Summer. We lived by the coast then and I would have only been six or seven anyway."

Caw had been back to the park only once in the previous two months and that was to get his meagre belongings from the old nest. As they got close, he found himself thinking how much his life had changed in such a short space of time. When he had lived in the tree-house, the world of ferals had been as much a mystery to him as it was to Selina. He had barely spoken to another human being.

Lydia Strickham and her family had changed all that.

There were lights on in the Strickham house when they arrived outside. Caw remembered what Lydia had said about her dad getting fired and how they might have to move. He felt a prickle of apprehension as they approached the front door. The first time he had come here for dinner, he had been struck almost dumb with nerves. His mind wandered ahead, to whether or not he was going to tell Mrs Strickham about the stone. The Midnight Stone, Mr Silk had called it. Quaker had told him not to. *Your mother would have told you the same –* that's what he'd said. Could that be true? Caw wasn't sure.

He raised his hand to knock, when Shimmer flew over the top of the house.

She's not alone. The man's with her.

Caw paused. "Mr Strickham."

"Why don't we go to Crumb instead?" said Pip. "He'll know what to—"

"No," said Caw. He could only imagine the pigeon feral's face if he found out what Selina and Caw had been up to. As it was, he was pretty sure he'd seen at least two pigeons following them a mile back. Crumb could wait.

Pip scuffed his feet sulkily.

"What's the problem with Mr Strickham?" asked Selina.

"He doesn't know his wife is a feral," said Caw. He thought for a moment. "We'll have to wait."

"It's freezing," said Selina.

Caw realised she was right. His clothes were still soaked from the fall into the river and the cold air seeped right through them.

"Let's go round the back," he said.

They scaled the walls at the rear of the house and dropped into the garden. Caw knew Lydia's room was on the second floor. Her curtains were closed, but her light was on.

"Screech, can you knock for us?"

A moment later, after the crow had tapped the window with his beak, Lydia's curtains drew back. When she saw Caw and his friends in the garden, she looked shocked, then angry. The curtains fell again.

"So she's your friend, is she?" asked Selina.

"I hope so," said Caw. It looked like Lydia was still smarting from their conversation at the funeral.

"Now we *have* to go back to the church," said Pip.

Caw was about to agree, reluctantly, when the back door opened a crack. Lydia peered out. "You'd better come in quietly," she said.

Caw and the others tiptoed inside, then up the stairs and into Lydia's bedroom. The walls were covered in animal posters. She closed the door behind them and looked at their damp clothes. "You look like you've been swimming," she said bluntly. "Is this the girl you told me about?"

"Hi, my name's Selina," she said, holding out her hand. "I like your bedroom, by the way. It's... cute."

"Lydia," said Lydia, not taking the hand. "So I guess your scavenging trip didn't go according to plan."

Caw opened his jacket, and took out a soggy packet of crushed biscuits.

Lydia rolled her eyes. "I hope it was worth it."

There was another tap at the window and Caw saw all three crows waiting there.

"They want to come in," he said.

Lydia opened the window and the crows flapped into the room.

Weird wallpaper, said Screech, inspecting the wall decorations. *Why no crows?*

"What's he saying?" said Lydia.

"He likes your posters," said Caw.

He explained what had happened down by the river, leaving out any mention of the stone. Lydia's face began to soften a little.

"You should have let me come with you," she said.

She nodded at Selina. "So is she a feral too?"

"No," said Caw. "Lydia, we need to speak to your mum."

Lydia's eyes drifted to his foot and she winced. "Caw, you're bleeding on my carpet."

Caw looked down too and saw a trail of blood dripping from his ankle. "Oh! Sorry!"

Lydia threw him a tissue from her bedside table and Caw gingerly rolled up his trouser leg. His calf and ankle were covered in puncture marks.

"Those look painful," said a voice. They all jumped.

Mrs Strickham was standing in the doorway, wearing a dressing gown.

"Mum! You could have knocked!" said Lydia.

"I could say the same for our guests," said Mrs Strickham. "Who is this young lady?" Her tone was disapproving.

"My name is Selina," she said, looking slightly afraid.

Caw tried to regain his composure. "I'm sorry, I brought her here," he said. "We didn't know where else to go. I... we had to tell her who we are."

Mrs Strickham glared at him. "You told her about ferals?"

Caw opened his mouth, then closed it again. His cheeks were burning.

"Hmm," said Mrs Strickham. She flashed a suspicious look at Selina, then cocked her head at Caw's leg. "Rat bites? Does that mean you've met the delightful Ms Pinkerton?"

Caw nodded. "Down by the docks," he said. "We were attacked by a moth feral too."

"Mr Silk?" said Mrs Strickham. "We weren't sure if he was still around. So what did they want?"

Caw hesitated, with Quaker's words running through his head. He'd said that the stone was the crow feral's burden. Would she take it away from him?

All at once, Caw made up his mind. He couldn't tell Mrs Strickham about it now – not in front of Lydia and

76

Pip. Not in front of Selina. He tried not to break eye contact as he lied. "I don't know," he said.

"Yes you do!" said Pip. "Isn't it obvious?"

Caw felt the blood rush from his face. Did Pip somehow know what he had in his pocket?

"The Crow's Beak!" said Pip. "The moth feral said to hand it over, didn't he?"

"Oh... oh yes," said Caw.

"But the Spinning Man's gone, isn't he?" said Lydia. "Even if they could cut a gateway to the Land of the Dead, they still couldn't bring him back. So what good is the Crow's Beak to them?"

"Good question," said her mother. "Whatever they're planning, they can't be allowed to have it."

"Perhaps we should go..." Caw began, but Mrs Strickham cut him off with a raised finger.

"Absolutely not. If Pinkerton and Silk are out there, I've no choice but to insist you stay here. You and the girl." She threw another icy glance at Selina. "Just make sure you keep the noise down. I'd rather not have to explain to Lydia's father why we are taking in waifs and strays. In the morning, we will work out what to do about all this."

"We could call a council of ferals," said Pip.

Mrs Strickham turned on him fiercely. "I'll let you know when I need your advice," she said. "Now, get some sleep."

After Mrs Strickham had closed the door behind her, Selina sighed.

"I thought *my* mum was strict," she said.

"She's just worried," said Caw.

"Both of you stop talking about my mum," snapped Lydia. She pointed to the sofa at the other side of the room. "Someone can have that. The other two will have to take the floor. There are blankets in the wardrobe."

What about us? said Shimmer.

Lydia turned towards the crow's squawk. "If that crow just said what I think it did, there are a lot of perfectly good branches outside."

That's animal cruelty, said Glum.

Still, Caw went to the window and opened it. "Go on, you three. Keep watch for me."

The crows flew out into the night. As Caw closed the window again, he caught the shadow of a fox lurking in the garden below.

I should have known there's no sneaking up on Velma Strickham, he thought, smiling to himself. She might be severe, but she was the best ally they had.

Selina took the sofa, and Caw lay down next to Pip on the carpet. Crumb would be wondering what was going on, but at least he knew they were safe.

It wasn't long before Caw heard the mouse feral's slow breathing, and Lydia's too. He wasn't sure if Selina was asleep or not. As he shifted to look, he felt the stone dig into his side.

Perhaps he could sneak out of the room now and

find Mrs Strickham. He could trust her, couldn't he? He propped himself up on to his elbows, ready to stand, but something stopped him.

Whatever the stone was, whatever it *did*, it was dangerous. Caw was sure of that. The moth feral had mentioned a woman, hadn't he? He said *she* wanted it. And it couldn't be a coincidence that Quaker had mentioned a "she" too.

She's watching us, even now. Who was this unknown enemy? Another feral, surely.

The Midnight Stone, Mr Silk had called it. Just a name, or some clue to its powers?

Caw shuddered. Night had always been his friend, but something told him that this stone was to be feared. In which case, why did his mother have it, and what could it possibly mean for him?

Caw let his hand enclose the cold stone, and his thoughts turned dark and confused. A knot of heartburn made it hurt to breathe. Something was wrong. Normally he took comfort from the crows' presence. Even when they weren't speaking, he could sense them on the borders of his consciousness. But now his mind searched and found only blankness. He was gripped by the unmistakable fear they had abandoned him.

All of a sudden, a memory sprang up. He'd been only five years old, no more, a time soon after the crows had taken him in. Back then he could do little for himself and had relied on the birds completely for worms, grubs, or whatever else they could bring him. It had been a storm-filled, winter night and the crows had not returned from their forage. Hungry, alone and cold, he'd felt a terror like nothing before. He remembered clearly the nest filled with his own throat-wrenching howls and the hot tears of despair flowing uncontrollably from his eyes...

Hardly able to breathe, Caw stood up and stumbled to the window, tugging back the curtains, sure the crows would not be there.

But they were. The three birds stood huddled side by side on the garden wall. Caw pushed open the window a fraction and drew a long breath of cool air. Glum tipped his head at Caw quizzically.

Everything OK? he said in a soft warble.

Caw allowed himself a couple of seconds to recover, then gave the crow a thumbs-up. The feeling passed, and his heart returned to its normal rhythm.

Letting the curtains drop back into place, he crept back to his bedding and lay down. As he adjusted his clothes, he felt the stone again, only this time he found himself unwilling to touch it.

This object was capable of great evil, an evil he couldn't yet begin to comprehend.

But one thing was certain. Until he knew the truth, it was an evil he would face alone.

Chapter 6

*T*he only sound was the gentle *creaking of branches as the nest swayed slightly. In the sky above, snow fell like ash, coating the trees. But as the flakes landed in the nest they melted into non-existence. Caw wasn't cold. He looked at his hand in front of him. In the centre of his palm lay the stone. Somehow its blackness seemed radiant, filling the nest with light and warmth.*

"Hello, Jack," said a kind voice.

Caw glanced up and his heart leapt. His mother sat opposite him, smiling. Her skin was pale, and her hair too – almost white. Even her eyelashes seemed to carry flecks of frost.

"You're here," he said. "But how?"

"In the Land of the Dead, many things are possible," she replied.

Caw looked again at the stone.

"You must keep it secret," said his mother. She reached

out with a delicate white hand and folded his fingers over the stone. "It is yours to bear alone, my son."

Caw felt the warmth of the stone passing along his veins.

"What is it?" he asked.

His mother flinched and drew her hand away. Her eyes widened.

"Go!" she said, standing and knocking over the chair on which she sat.

Caw began to panic. "But I want to stay with you," he said.

"He's coming, Jack," she said. "Go now."

Caw rushed to the hatch at the bottom of the nest and flung it open. At the base of the tree, a dark slick was closing in on the trunk, making the snow black.

Spiders. Millions of them.

"Don't let him have it, Jack," said his mother. She was pressing her body against the edge of the nest, trembling. "He must not have it."

Caw crouched, transfixed, as the spiders pooled at the bottom of the trunk, piling over one another in a torrent. They began to climb, rising in a black, shuffling tide. Unstoppable.

Caw slammed the hatch down and drew across the bar to bolt it. "Tell me what it is!" he said. "Why does he want it?"

But when he looked up again, his mother had gone.

He was alone. The nest was empty and the snow was beginning to settle.

Bang.

The hatch shook and the nest trembled.

Bang Bang Bang.

Something was pounding on the other side. He knew what it was. He knew who it was.

The Spinning Man.

His breath ragged, he climbed to the edge of the nest. He could still get away. He could fly. He was the crow feral – the sky was his friend. All he had to do was change.

Bang Bang Bang.

Crash.

The hatch splintered and a spindly hand reached through, the fingers flexing like spider-legs.

Caw threw himself off the edge of the nest, spreading his arms and willing them to become wings.

But they did not.

Fear ripped out his heart as he fell, branches whipping his skin.

He hit the ground with a jolt, and then all was still.

He lay on his back in the snow. There was no pain, but he couldn't feel his body at all. His mind drifted, untethered, and his eyes took in the sight of a swirling winter sky.

Then he heard the footsteps. Soft crunches, each one louder than the one before.

The Spinning Man was coming.

Caw clamped his eyes shut so as not to see the object of his terror.

The footsteps stopped.

"Open them," whispered a soft voice. A voice laced with cruelty.

Caw tried to turn away, but a hand gripped his chin and held it steady.

"Look at me," said the voice.

Caw's eyes obeyed, though he willed them not to.

The Spinning Man stood over him, his face scarred beneath the falling spikes of black hair. Caw begged his body to move, but it did not.

"I want it," said his enemy. The Spinning Man's eyes were spider eyes, shining silver, reflecting Caw's terrified face.

Caw shook his head as much as he could in the strong grip. He could not give up the stone his mother had entrusted to him.

The Spinning Man knelt over him, so that his face was just a foot from Caw's. His skin was a smooth sheen. Too smooth, Caw thought. With the long fingers of his free hand, the Spinning Man reached up and pressed his fingertips into his own face. His blackened nails bit into his pale flesh.

Caw's heart thumped in horror as the spider feral began to tear his face away, peeling the skin from his *skull. It was a mask, he realised. This creature wasn't the Spinning Man at all, but someone else.*

Caw closed his eyes, terrified of what lay beneath...

A dim light was seeping through his eyelids. Caw blinked. At first he was confused, but as the nightmare faded, the previous night came flooding back. He looked sideways and saw the others still had their eyes closed. Selina was frowning a little in her sleep. Pip was huddled in a ball.

Caw felt a stab of guilt. Even if Crumb's spies had seen them come to the house, he'd still be worried, especially for the mouse feral.

From outside came the sound of a car engine. The bedroom door opened and Mrs Strickham was standing there, already wearing a dark coat.

"Good morning, everyone. It's time to go."

"Go where?" asked Caw, sitting up.

"My husband is at a meeting all morning," said Lydia's mother, turning away. "I've called a gathering. It starts in an hour."

"So you followed my advice," said Pip, puffing out his narrow chest.

Mrs Strickham's lips twitched into the ghost of a smile as she left the room.

Caw staggered to his feet and followed her. "Wait," he said, lowering his voice. "What about Selina?"

Mrs Strickham raised an eyebrow. "She'll have to come with us. Now she knows about the ferals, she's a liability. We can't let her out of our sight."

Caw detected an accusation in her tone and he blushed.

"I'm sorry," he said.

Mrs Strickham's face softened and she touched his arm. "Don't worry," she said. "We can deal with the problem later. Now, we didn't get a chance to speak properly at Emily's funeral. How has Crumb been treating you? Your training's going well, I hear."

Caw hesitated for a moment. He'd assumed Mrs Strickham had no contact with Crumb, but now she sounded like she knew what was going on at the church. "It's hard," he said. "But I'm getting better every day."

"Good," she said. "And have you managed to turn into a crow again?"

Caw shook his head, remembering his failed attempt from the day before, outside Quaker's house.

Mrs Strickham nodded. "You're lucky you even managed to do it once," she said. "I've been trying to become a fox for years." She squeezed his arm tighter. "You have a gift, Caw. Keep trying."

Caw's heart swelled momentarily with pride as she walked away down the stairs, but as he turned to go back into the bedroom, he remembered the other thing she had said.

What exactly had she meant by "dealing" with the Selina 'problem'?

Mrs Strickham led them to the door of a large taxi. It was driven by a young Asian man with piercings in his lip and dark circles under his eyes. Caw was pretty sure he'd never seen the man before. Going by Lydia's frown, neither had she.

"To the zoo," said Mrs Strickham through the window.

The driver's hands tightened on the wheel.

"Please," said Mrs Strickham. "I know it will be hard."

The driver nodded. "If we must, Mrs S."

As Pip climbed into the back, he noticed the mouse feral give the driver the briefest of smiles. *They know each other too. Is he a feral?* Caw and Selina got in the back too, Mrs Strickham going up in the front beside the driver. Caw nodded through the window to the crows perched on the wall of the park opposite. "Follow us," he called.

Where are we going? said Screech.

Just do as he says, muttered Glum.

Caw squeezed in further to make room for Lydia. With four in the back, she could only just manage to close the door behind her.

Immediately the taxi turned in the road and sped off through the city.

"So how come I haven't heard of Mr Silk or Pinkerton before?" said Pip. "Crumb never mentioned them."

Caw sat straighter, hairs bristling. Whoever this driver was, he was definitely one of them, otherwise Pip wouldn't mention the ferals.

"They weren't around in the Dark Summer," said Mrs Strickham. "They were always close to... well, it doesn't matter really. They're back now."

Caw caught the snag in her voice. *She's keeping something back*, he thought.

"Close to who?" he asked.

Mrs Strickham didn't answer for a few seconds, but Caw watched her reflection in the wing mirror of the car. Her fingers rested on the side of her face and a flash of a frown creased her forehead as she stared into the middle distance.

"The Mother of Flies," she said quietly.

The cab driver shifted uncomfortably in his seat.

The name meant nothing to Caw, yet there was something in the way Mrs Strickham said it and in her troubled expression that sent a cold thrill through his veins. Selina leant forward to listen.

"Ha!" said Pip. "The fly feral. No way! She's a myth. Crumb says no one's ever even seen her."

Her.

Caw thought again of Pinkerton's words – *she wants it* – and a shiver ran down his spine.

"Crumb is entitled to his opinions," said Mrs Strickham.

"So she didn't fight in the Dark Summer?" asked Caw.

Mrs Strickham sighed. "It's a long story," she said. "Perhaps Felix Quaker could tell you the details, but for generations, the fly ferals were spurned. You have to understand, people were different back then. There was a kind of order among the ferals and the fly talkers were always looked down on. I suppose it started off as suspicion, because of what flies are – they feed on what is rotten, scavenging from the dead. But even in my father's time, no one really mixed with the fly line."

"I heard they moved away from Blackstone before I was born," said the driver.

Caw glanced around for any sign of the man's creatures, but there was nothing obvious in the cab.

"So is this Mother of Flies real or not?" said Lydia, impatiently.

"I don't know," said her mother. "I've certainly never seen her myself. But it is said the fly ferals are always women. If there is no female heir, the gift passes a generation. There's never been a male fly talker."

"My mother used to tell us stories about the fly ferals to make us behave," said the driver. "She said they could sneak into any room as long as there was a hole big enough for a single fly. My sister and I used to block up the keyhole to our bedroom at night just in case the Mother of Flies came for us."

Caw kept silent, a sense of unease creeping across

his skin. Quaker had been afraid of a woman too. *She's watching us, even now...*

"Is there any news on your sister, Chen?" said Mrs Strickham. Caw got the impression she was pleased to change the subject.

The pierced man shook his head. "Nothing," he said.

"Won't there be people at the zoo?" asked Selina.

"No," said Mrs Strickham. "It finally closed its doors last week. All the remaining animals have been shipped off to other cities."

"Oh," said Lydia. "Now I'll never get the chance to go!"

"It wasn't that great anyway," said Selina. "Just for little kids, really."

Caw felt Lydia stiffen. "How old are *you*, anyway?" she said, not even looking at Selina.

"Fifteen," said Selina. "What about you?"

Lydia didn't reply.

It began to rain. Chen took several narrow backstreets to avoid the worst of the traffic and pulled up around the rear entrance of Blackstone Zoo. There were signs nailed up saying the land had been bought by "Futura Developments". Caw's crows were already perched on one waiting for them.

Lydia's mother stepped out with an umbrella, opened the gate a fraction and beckoned them inside. Chen followed, pulling a hood over his head, and the others trailed behind him.

"This place is special to the ferals," said Mrs Strickham. "Back in the Dark Summer we used it as a night base sometimes, until the Spinning Man found out and laid a trap. Many good ferals died. Madeleine's father – the squirrel talker. Sylvia, the bear talker."

"My father too," said Chen quietly.

So that's why he hadn't wanted to come here, thought Caw.

Mrs Strickham led them down a tiled passage beside an empty concrete pool with faded pictures of penguins on the side, catching fish. As they went, Caw noticed two foxes silently slip into their wake, summoned, it seemed, from thin air.

Selina, Caw noticed, was quiet and pale. The last twenty-four hours must have been so strange for her, he thought. He gave her an encouraging smile, and waited for her to catch up.

Mrs Strickham stopped at a door with a sign that said "Zoo Keepers Only". She pushed it open and led them across an empty room, then through another set of double doors. They found themselves beside a pond of scum-covered rainwater surrounded by fake boulders. The odour of rotten fish lingered in the air. Caw realised they were actually inside the old penguin enclosure.

Crumb was waiting, huddled under a canopy, along

with several other figures – ferals from the funeral, and a few others besides. Over two dozen easily. Caw felt a tingle of excitement. He'd never seen so many together before. But as he scanned the faces, the thrill quickly waned. Was this all of them? It was hardly the army he'd imagined from the Dark Summer. Birds flapped around and settled on the pool's edge, and there were several dogs of different species. A scaly lizard slithered across the floor, flicking a black tongue. Two men, both in their sixties, embraced warmly. At their feet a rabbit sniffed a tortoise that had retreated into its shell.

Crumb rushed forward and embraced Pip. Over the boy's head, he glared at Caw.

"I can't stop you sneaking off, but you should leave Pip out of it."

Caw felt his cheeks heating up as Pip pulled away. "Don't blame Caw – I followed him."

Crumb looked like he was about say something else, when Racklen called out. "So what's this all about?"

"Yeah, what's the deal?" said a woman. There was a lizard perched on her shoulder. "It's dangerous, coming here. Draws attention."

Several others joined the rumblings of discontent, but Mrs Strickham raised her hands and the crowd fell silent. Caw noticed two black shapes swoop from above. Chen opened his jacket and they landed inside, hanging upside down and squeaking. Bats! Chen grinned and let his jacket fall closed again.

"Our enemies are resurfacing," said Mrs Strickham. "Last night, the moth talker and the rat feral attacked our friend Caw."

The eyes of the assembly all focused on him, expectant.

Caw cleared his throat. He could feel his cheeks getting hot as they stared at him. Many of these people would have fought alongside his parents in the Dark Summer. Others would have lost parents in that conflict. He could feel the stone in his pocket, heavier than ever.

It is yours to bear alone...

"Caw?" said Crumb. "Just tell us what happened."

And so he did, mostly with his eyes downcast. He told them he'd been scavenging with a friend, about the boat, and about the attack. He told them about the rats and the moths.

But he didn't tell them about the stone.

He told himself he wasn't lying – he was just choosing what to share. As he finished his tale, he dared to look up, and though he could feel that most believed him, there was puzzlement in several pairs of eyes.

"I think I'd be dead if it weren't for Pip and his mice," he added. "They saved my life."

That seemed to sway any suspicion, and everyone's attention turned to Pip, who stood blushing beside Crumb.

"We think they wanted the Crow's Beak!" said the mouse feral boldly. "We need to find out what they're planning and strike back!"

A few of the ferals nodded, or muttered to themselves, but the response was far from overwhelming.

Racklen pointed a finger at Selina. "So she's the *friend*, I suppose. I don't trust humans."

Selina drew herself up. "My name's Selina," she said. "And *I* don't know if I trust strange people who talk to animals!"

Her words were met with a chorus of angry shouts, but Selina stood defiant until they died down.

Chen screwed up his face. "None of this makes sense. Why now? Why Pinkerton and Mr Silk? They must have been following the crow..." He stopped, twitching his head. "Wait. I hear something!"

Screech and the crows took off, as well as several other birds.

The next moment Caw heard a squeal of brakes and slamming doors.

Cops! cried Glum from above. Other birds squawked and the ferals looked at each other in alarm. How had the police found them?

Shouts and hurried footsteps sounded from all around, then something sailed over the top of the penguin enclosure and slid, rattling, across the tiles, streaming smoke. Another followed.

"Smoke grenades!" said Mrs Strickham. "Run, everyone!"

Caw's feet wouldn't budge. Where was he supposed to run to?

"Freeze!"

"Don't move!"

The voices came from shadows around the perimeter of the enclosure. Through the drifting smoke, Caw could make out several dozen cops in SWAT gear, all levelling weapons at the ferals.

Crumb grabbed Caw in one hand and dragged Pip with the other, back towards the doors through which they'd entered.

"Wait!" Caw shouted. "Selina!"

But Crumb wasn't letting go. Caw heard the growls of several animals, and shrieking birds flapped upwards through the smoke. Two of Velma Strickham's foxes leapt up towards the edge of the enclosure, baring their teeth. "Hey!" cried one of the cops. Then there was a sudden crack of a gunshot.

"Hold your fire! Stand down!" someone shouted, but in the panic it seemed too late. More shots exploded. Caw saw the animals – birds and rodents and small mammals – falling on the police as bullets sprayed everywhere, smacking into tiles and whistling overhead. Screech was turning mid-air, when his body twisted violently and he plummeted.

"No!" shouted Caw, but Crumb thrust him through the doors. Caw saw Mrs Strickham was already ahead, with Lydia in tow. But where was Selina? They burst into the corridor and ran towards the exit. At the far end, Caw finally managed to pull free of Crumb. "We can't leave the others!" he said.

Mrs Strickham stood in his way. "Don't you see?" she said. "It was a trap! They must have found out we were planning to meet here. Follow me now or we're all dead."

"No, Caw's right!" said Pip, shrugging so that Crumb was left holding only his jacket. The mouse feral ran back towards the battle, ignoring Crumb's panicked shouts. Crumb and Caw tried to go after him, but several foxes barred their path.

"I already told you. You're coming with us," said Mrs Strickham sternly.

"Come back!" Crumb cried after Pip, but the mouse feral had already disappeared back into the enclosure. Caw thought of jumping the foxes, but they pressed too close. Lydia took Caw's arm gently. "Come on," she said, as the whip-cracking of bullets and the wailing of ferals and animals rose to a cacophony.

The foxes forced Caw and Crumb further from the enclosure. Dazed, Caw turned and stumbled after Lydia. It had all happened so quickly. Maybe Selina had already managed to get out?

Mrs Strickham led them up a set of stairs, towards

a deserted café full of dusty tables and scrawled menu boards. One side was all glass, opening up to a view over the penguin enclosure.

"Cease fire! Cease fire!" said a woman's voice from below. "Contain them!"

As the gunfire ended, Caw crept to the edge to see. The smoke was clearing, but the sight in the tiled pit was terrible. All the ferals were clumped together in a circle, coughing and clutching tight to one another. Many were crying, and one woman was being cradled by Racklen, blood dripping from her arm. Caw saw one of the old men clutching a limp ferret to his chest, his hands covered in blood. A few animals lay scattered on the ground – including several birds. Caw searched for Screech, but he couldn't see him.

The ferals were surrounded by armed police wearing masks. More officers crouched on the balcony above. A short woman dressed in a fitted black suit and white blouse paced between them, her heels clicking on the ground. She looked calm and poised, her hair tied back with not a strand out of place. She wore scarlet lipstick and matching nail polish.

"Arrest them all," she said.

"That's Cynthia Davenport," said Mrs Strickham. "She's the new Police Commissioner of Blackstone."

"The one who sacked Dad?" said Lydia.

The police walked forward cautiously, but none of

the ferals offered any resistance, nor summoned their animals.

"My boy..." muttered Crumb. "I can't let them take him."

"This gang has been on the loose for years," Cynthia Davenport was saying to the man beside her. "They're responsible for half the crimes across Blackstone." She clicked her fingers at the officers below. "No, not her! She's the one who led us to them."

Caw strained his eyes and saw Selina walking out of the midst of the ferals, going to stand at the policewoman's side. She looked unsure of herself, scared even.

"Hello, darling," said the woman, trying to put her arm around Selina.

Caw almost choked.

"She knows her!" said Lydia.

"You said you wouldn't hurt them," said Selina, shaking off the embrace.

"I didn't *want* to hurt anyone," said Cynthia Davenport. "But we have the situation under control now. Those with injuries will be treated properly."

"Traitor!" said Mrs Strickham, her face aghast – a mixture of bewilderment and anger. Caw could hardly believe it.

"We need to find the ringleader too," Commissioner Davenport continued, looking away from Selina back to the surrounded ferals. "He's about thirteen, dark hair, dressed in black."

Caw wondered who she was talking about. For some reason, the others were all looking at him. Wait – hold on – surely they didn't think...

"His name is Jack Carmichael, but his gang name is Caw."

Caw froze, his heart knocking against his ribcage. None of this made sense. A ringleader of what? It had to be some sort of mistake.

"Mum, I don't think this is right," said Selina. *She's the commissioner's daughter!* thought Caw. "He's not –"

"And take her somewhere safe," interrupted her mother.

Caw kept very still. Selina turned and walked away as a female police officer approached her. He watched them hurry under an exit sign, out of sight.

"We need to get out of here," said Mrs Strickham, as the police began to spread out below.

"What about the others?" said Crumb, his voice strained with anger. Caw shuffled backwards and knocked into a chair. The scraping on the floor was tiny, but at the same instant, Cynthia Davenport's eyes flicked up towards their hiding place.

She pointed a finger at the window. "There," she said.

Two armed SWAT members began to run towards the café. Others levelled their weapons.

"Come out with your hands up!" one shouted.

Caw ducked out of sight. He looked at Lydia and Crumb, crouching beside him. Mrs Strickham shook her head grimly.

"Clear the glass!" shouted a man's voice. Bullets hit the window with loud cracks, shattering the glass into thousands of fragments that rained down on top of them.

"Take cover!" cried Mrs Strickham as they heard the boots of the men pounding towards the stairs to the café.

But Caw didn't listen. He knew exactly what to do. Lifting a hand, he felt his power surge, and just as the gun-carrying cops reached the steps, a black mass descended from the open sky over the penguin enclosure. The crows swooped in front, above and around the cops like a shroud, holding them back, knocking them to the ground. The men thrashed madly beneath the thumping wings and raking talons.

"Come on! There must be a way out the back," said Mrs Strickham.

They all jumped over the café counter and into a kitchen on the other side. Sure enough, a fire door led to another set of steps descending to the zoo car park. Mrs Strickham led the way, with Lydia and Caw following right behind, until Caw noticed Crumb wasn't with them. He ran back into the café and saw Crumb standing by the broken window, moving his hands in a way Caw recognised from their training. Controlling his pigeons. Bullets zinged into the café, smashing glasses and cups on shelves. Caw dashed forward in a crouch and grabbed Crumb's belt.

"Come on!" he said. "There's no time!"

Crumb resisted, pulling back with all his weight. "I can't leave him!" He clenched his fists and flung his hands out.

Caw dared to look over the broken window and saw several pigeons trying to pluck Pip out from the melee, but the police were holding him down. "It's hopeless!" said Caw. "We have to go. We'll get him back – I promise!" At last Crumb allowed himself to be pulled away.

Outside, Lydia and her mother were waiting by Chen's taxi. Mrs Strickham jumped into the front seat and pulled down the visor. A set of keys dropped into her lap. "Get in!" she said.

Glum and Shimmer landed on the bonnet.

Is Screech with you? asked Glum. *We lost him...*

Caw didn't know what to say. He couldn't tell them yet. "Follow us," he said. "And keep a lookout."

They piled into the cab together, slamming the doors. Then, with a roar of the engine and squeal of rubber, they left the zoo – and Pip – behind.

Chapter 7

Tears rolled freely down Crumb's cheeks and his shoulders shook. "I left him," he said.

Caw had never seen the older feral so broken. He placed an arm awkwardly over Crumb's rangy shoulders.

"If you had been captured too, he wouldn't stand a chance," Caw said as the car skidded around a corner. "At least this way we can –"

"It should have been me!" snapped Crumb, angrily throwing off the arm.

Outside the window, the two crows were doing as Caw had asked and watching from the air. Mrs Strickham drove fast, leaning forward with both hands gripping the wheel and checking the mirrors every couple of seconds. She took a route two blocks back from the river before crossing over. From time to time, they heard sirens, but never close by.

Caw felt sick. This was all his fault. Selina had

completely duped him. He tried to think back over their previous encounters, searching for clues. His nausea redoubled – it all added up. Her being at his parents' house, her questions about where he lived now... she'd been working for her mother all along, acting as a police spy.

How hadn't he seen it – how had he let himself be taken in? He knew exactly how – he'd been too busy thinking about the stone and wondering what it meant. The depth of his own stupidity gnawed at his stomach.

The city outside the car windows was going about its business as always – people in suits heading to work, or carrying cups of coffee through the streets – and the normality of it made Caw feel even more like he was living in some sort of nightmare. Mrs Strickham pulled in beside the run-down church and they all got out, Glum and Shimmer landing beside them.

We weren't followed, said Shimmer.

"Thank you," said Caw numbly.

Glum's eyes looked empty. Despite their constant bickering, Caw knew that Glum loved Screech like a son.

Caw's neck prickled and he looked up to find the others all staring at him. Crumb, leaning forward, hands on the roof on the car, glared angrily, while Mrs Strickham was staring over Lydia's head as they embraced.

"I'm so sorry," said Caw, then wished he hadn't. The words fell leaden from his lips, totally inadequate.

Crumb slapped a hand on the car. "I *told* you, Caw. I *told* you. Don't trust humans. They're not like us."

"Hey!" said Lydia, breaking from her mother. "He couldn't have known, OK?"

Caw's heart lifted a fraction to hear his friend back him up, but he knew Crumb was right.

"That's the point!" said Crumb, turning on her. "That's why we keep to ourselves. Because it's better to be secretive and safe."

"Calm down," said Mrs Strickham. She seemed to have recovered some of her composure. "The police have our friends, but what can they actually charge them with? None of them will show their powers now. All isn't lost. Why don't we go inside?" Caw noticed several foxes already gathering by the door.

"Don't blame yourself," said Lydia, as they shuffled into the church. "You weren't stupid. Selina tricked us all."

Caw felt numb. "You don't have to say that," he said.

"If I could get my hands on her..." said Lydia.

"Well, we can't," said Mrs Strickham.

Crumb hurried to the stairs.

"Where are you going?" said Mrs Strickham. "We need to come up with—"

"I need a minute," said Crumb. "Just leave me be."

Mrs Strickham shook her head in frustration.

"I don't understand," said Lydia. "Why did she want to arrest Caw? He's not a criminal."

"People always distrust what they don't understand," said Lydia's mother. "Perhaps it's something to do with our fight against the Spinning Man's disciples, Mamba and Roach. Caw was arrested along with them, remember, at the sewing factory. He would have been taken to prison if he hadn't escaped from custody."

Caw shook his head, puzzled. Could that really be the reason for the carnage at the zoo?

It only made him feel worse. On that occasion he'd escaped the police handcuffs with Pip's help, and yet now Pip was in trouble because of him.

What about Screech? said Shimmer on the back of a pew. *Maybe he was injured. They'll probably leave him there. Won't they? Should we go back?*

The memory of his crow falling to the ground hit Caw like a smack in the gut as he followed the others into the nave. Screech was the bravest, most foolhardy crow he'd ever known. He'd almost got himself killed countless times, and still he had kept throwing himself into danger.

We can't just abandon him, said Glum. *Let me go back and look.*

Me too! said Shimmer.

"It's too dangerous," said Caw.

We're not asking you to come with us, said Shimmer. *We can do it on our own.*

"That's not what I meant," said Caw. "I need you here. If anything happens to you too—"

I have to know, said Glum, *if he's...*

Caw saw his own reflection in the silky black orb of Glum's eye. He looked haggard, drained.

But it gave him an idea. He turned to Mrs Strickham, who was resting her hand on a fox's head. "I need your help."

"With what?" she said.

"You said you could get inside the minds of your foxes," Caw continued. "Show me how. If I can get inside Screech, I'll know if he's still alive."

The fox feral frowned, clearly doubtful.

"Mum, try," said Lydia.

"Very well," said Mrs Strickham. She unfastened her coat and sat cross-legged on the floor. Her foxes all lay down on their bellies a few metres away. "Take a seat, Caw. The rest of you, please be quiet. It takes immense concentration."

Caw sat opposite Lydia's mother. He didn't feel confident.

"Close your eyes and try to relax," she said. "Empty your thoughts."

He found it hard. Whenever he shut his eyelids, scenes from the battle at the zoo replayed themselves. The SWAT team, the barrel flares from their guns, the terrified ferals cowering. And Selina's face as she stood beside her mother.

"I can sense your anger," said Mrs Strickham. "Caw, you can't do this unless you let go."

Caw shooed the thoughts away, but almost at once others crowded in to fill their place. That first meeting with Selina in his old bedroom, the way he'd managed to make her laugh. The rush of pride as she'd said they should meet up again. He'd fallen for it without question, and all the time she'd been laughing not at his feeble jokes, but at the fool she was making of him.

Caw, relax, said Glum. *Please, for Screech.*

Caw took another deep breath and pushed Selina from his mind. He tried to imagine a black ball of emptiness in his brain, impervious, keeping everything at bay.

"OK, now concentrate on the crow," said Mrs Strickham. "Speak his name inside your head, think of his form and nothing else."

Caw began to do what she said.

Screech... Screech... Screech... He imagined the crow in happier times, seated on the edge of the nest.

"His spirit is out there," said Mrs Strickham. "Find it."

Screech...

He thought of him swooping down to drink from a puddle.

Screech...

He remembered how he had gobbled up whole chips without even chewing.

Screech...

It happened quite suddenly. The black image in Caw's mind began to break apart, collapsing into spots of bright light. It felt as though his mind was rending into two, then turning over slowly to open another plane of thought, ancient and alien. The crow disappeared and a different scene began to coalesce. The image seemed curved, bent out of shape, but as the light faded, Caw saw the face of the Police Commissioner, Cynthia Davenport. She held a compact mirror and was applying lipstick. Caw realised he was in the back of a car. There was no sign of Screech.

Cynthia Davenport stopped suddenly and turned to look right at him. Her cold grey eyes narrowed with curiosity.

"I was wondering when you'd come," she said.

Confused, Caw tried to speak, but all that came out was a crow's raucous cry. He looked left and right and saw, to his shock, two huge black wings held out, taut, and tied to what looked like the headrest of a car seat. One was crusted with dried blood and broken feathers. He felt suddenly trapped and tried to move. He flexed and heaved his shoulder joints and wished he hadn't. The wings strained and pain shot through his body. Now he understood what he was seeing. His body *was* the body of a crow.

He was inside Screech.

"Don't struggle," said Davenport softly.

Caw could feel his heart beating rapidly. What was going on? Why did the Police Commissioner have Screech in her car? Did she know about the ferals?

She lowered her face nearer to his. Now Caw saw her features closely, the resemblance to Selina was clear. They had the same flaring nose, porcelain skin and broad forehead. The eyes were completely different though – the mother's had no kindness or compassion. A squawk of pain escaped his beak.

"You're probably wondering what all this is about," she said.

The rear doors on either side of the car opened, and Caw flinched as Mr Silk climbed in from one side, Pinkerton from the other. The rat feral scratched her neck with dirty crooked nails. They knew Mrs Davenport? But...

Mr Silk settled into his seat and tipped his hat towards Selina's mother. "Ma'am," he said.

Light flooded over Caw's confused thoughts as he struggled to keep up with what he was seeing. His slow-burning dread sharpened into terror. They knew her. They were working for her. Which meant...

"Don't try to speak," said Cynthia Davenport. "Just listen very carefully. This is not a negotiation, or an idle threat. I have all your kind, and I've brought them to the prison where they belong. Bring me the stone by midnight, or I will kill them all. Involve your *friends* and they will die as well. Your choice is really quite simple, *crow talker*."

She smiled, as a small black insect, wings flickering, emerged from behind her ear. Caw watched in horror as it crawled across the perfectly smooth skin of her cheek and scurried up her nostril. She didn't even flinch.

It was her. It had to be. Cynthia Davenport – Selina's mother – was the Mother of Flies.

"And now," she said. "We have no more use for this creature. Are your rats hungry, Pinkerton?"

"A-a-always," said Pinkerton, her bloodshot eyes widening. "*Famished.*"

Caw felt his wings wrenched free in Cynthia Davenport's grip, as she and her cronies climbed from the car. Then the world jolted sideways as she hurled him through the air. He hit the ground and crumpled in agony. Staring at the tarmac, he tried to move on his injured wing, but waves of pain paralysed his body.

Cynthia Davenport looked down on him pitilessly, then her stiletto heels marched away, tip-tapping on the ground.

Caw panicked. Scurrying feet and four furred bodies surrounded him. The rats bared their teeth.

Get up! Caw urged.

He tried to use his talons to ward off the rats. One from behind must have darted forward, because suddenly his wing was being tugged violently. Teeth sank into his back. He flapped and flapped, crying out, but the rats clamped their jaws across his body. *They're tearing me apart!*

He felt lancing pain as feathers tore from his skin, and with each bite, Caw sensed his connection to Screech weakening. He focused his mind on the agony. He couldn't let go. He couldn't leave his friend.

But they were all over him. They were killing him. The stink of rat was overwhelming as their spittle coated his face and feathers, frantic with greed.

Then a white shape leapt screeching, into the fray, followed by another. Smaller than the rats, but just as vicious, an army of mice piled in. The teeth and claws let go and Caw rolled on to his back, talons wheeling helplessly. Through the blood and pain he saw rats trying to free themselves from the mice.

Caw realised this might be his only chance and he willed his crow body on to its feet. One of his legs was broken, he thought, hopping lopsidedly across the ground. But he forced all his strength into his aching wings and flapped. For the first three or four beats he only managed to drag himself across the tarmac, but then he was airborne, flapping wildly.

The ground dropped away and he saw the mice scattering from the prone bodies of four weakened rats. As he climbed higher, the wind cooled his wings and Blackstone Prison loomed into view. Several armoured vans were parked in a fenced yard, and police were unloading prisoners in handcuffs – the ferals. Caw swooped past and saw a face among them that was staring right at him. It was Pip, struggling in the hands of a police officer.

"Go Screech!" he shouted. "Tell Caw he's our only chance!"

The officer dragged him back into line.

Caw's eyes caught a flutter of movement in the air to his left. He'd barely turned to look properly when hundreds of flapping shapes fell over him like a blanket, clouding his vision. *Moths!* He batted through them with his wings, but with each stroke he felt more clustering on his wings, sapping his strength. It was the sound, dragging him downwards.

Got to get away!

Caw let his wings fold and gravity take him. He dropped away beneath the cloud of moths, then flapped hard, ignoring the pain, scattering the moths from his feathers as he gained speed. The insects followed, but he was quicker. Soon he was flying south, towards the river, the adrenaline seeping away and leaving only a dull ache across his wings. The city swept past and he sensed its updrafts like warm exhalations from a living creature. His crow eye bent the world so he could take in wide peripherals and the horizon all around.

The broken tower of St Francis came into view and Caw angled his wings to a glide. He tipped them to slow and dipped through the hole in the rafters. Pigeons scattered from his descent and he flapped through the long nave, over Mrs Strickham and Lydia.

It's Screech! he heard Glum cry.

Then he saw a boy sitting cross-legged on the floor, and he realised it was himself, staring with vacant eyes at nothing. He was home – he couldn't fly any more...

Caw snapped to attention just in time to see Screech land awkwardly and sprawl across the slabs on the church floor. Lydia rushed to the fallen crow, and Glum and Shimmer landed at his side.

Screech? said Shimmer.

Caw tried to stand, but everything felt wrong, and he staggered clumsily against an old pew. It took a few seconds for the pins and needles to fade from his legs and for his limbs to feel like his own again.

"You did it!" said Mrs Strickham. She took hold of his shoulders to keep him from falling.

Wake up, Screech, Glum was saying.

Caw struggled to find his voice and it came out as a croak. "It's her," he said. "Mrs Davenport. She's the Mother of Flies."

"What?" said Mrs Strickham.

Caw nodded. "Cynthia Davenport. I saw her. She's the fly feral."

Mrs Strickham gripped him more tightly. "How do you know?"

"There was a fly on her face. Pinkerton and Mr Silk were with her in a car. And now she's taken the ferals to the prison."

Screech was moving weakly. "Are you all right?" Caw asked him.

A bit wobbly, said the crow.

"What's going on?" asked Crumb, emerging from upstairs again. His eyes widened. "Is that Screech?"

Lydia was crouching beside the crow, slowly helping him extend his wing.

"The Mother of Flies is back in Blackstone," said Mrs Strickham. "She has our friends at the prison."

Crumb's skin went ashen. "You're not serious?"

"It's Cynthia Davenport," said Caw.

"But how can...?" said the pigeon feral. "Are you sure?"

Caw nodded. "It all fits. That's how Pinkerton and Mr Silk tracked me and Selina to the boat. I wouldn't have spotted a fly following me."

"Can't you see?" said Lydia. "It was Selina! She led you straight there!"

Caw felt sickened. Of course she had.

Mrs Strickham paced and Caw's mind churned the events over and over. Everything was starting to make sense. Somehow Cynthia Davenport had known that Caw would have the stone. So she planted Selina in his house to track him. The police at Quaker's must have been working for her too, trying to extract Caw's whereabouts from the cat feral.

"The Mother of Flies," murmured Crumb, with a

shudder. "What has that *creature* crawled back to Blackstone for?"

Caw's skin flushed and his mouth went dry. There was only one thing for it – he had to tell them. If his mother was here, would she have told him to stay silent? There was no way to tell. He had to make his own decisions. And he knew one thing for sure – secret or no secret, it wasn't just his own life at stake any more.

"She must be planning an attack on the city," said Mrs Strickham. "Why else would she have taken all the ferals into custody?"

"It isn't that," Caw said quietly.

Mrs Strickham turned her eyes on him. "Pardon?"

Caw swallowed. He could hardly breathe and his face was burning. The moment had come, and he didn't know what to say.

"I... I was going to..."

"Spit it out," said Crumb. "If you know something, tell us. Pip's in danger, Caw!"

And so, Caw told them everything he'd held back before, at the zoo, mostly looking at the floor. The words came out in a rush, from the first meeting with the stranger outside his house, to his meeting with Quaker, to the full story about the fight on the boat, and the Mother of Flies' ultimatum. The only thing he left out was his dream – how could that mean anything to them?

He expected anger, but when he did finally dare to

glance up, he saw that Crumb and Mrs Strickham were just puzzled.

"This man outside your house," said Mrs Strickham. "No hair, you say – none at all?"

"Not that I could see," said Caw.

Lydia's mother frowned. "It sounds like the worm feral. Was he very old?"

Caw shrugged. "It was hard to tell. But yes, he looked old and pale."

Mrs Strickham's frown deepened. "Bootlace, we used to call him when I was a girl. But he seemed like an old man even back then. He must be ancient if he's still alive now."

Caw remembered the worm Shimmer had prised from the earth just before he entered the house. "There was a worm! Perhaps it was just a coincidence, but..."

Mrs Strickham focused her grim stare on Caw again. "You should have told us all this before."

Caw felt his cheeks burning again. "I'm sorry. Quaker told me it was mine alone to look after. That my mother wouldn't want me to tell anyone about it."

"That old fool," muttered Crumb.

"So where is this stone?" asked Lydia, stiffly. Caw realised at once that she *was* angry at him. But could he blame her? He hadn't told her about the stone. After all the kindness she'd shown him, he'd kept it secret from her.

He reached into his pocket and slowly drew out the

stone. It looked plainer than before. Utterly lifeless and matt black. Everyone crowded closer.

"May I?" said Mrs Strickham, holding out her hand.

Caw placed it in her palm.

There was a sudden screeching and hissing. Caw spun round to see Mrs Strickham's foxes had leapt to their feet, hackles bristling across their backs. Mrs Strickham dropped the stone at once. "What on Earth…?" she said, staring at her hands.

"Mum?" said Lydia, looking up from beside Screech.

The foxes settled again and padded towards their mistress. They made soft mewling noises and strange, cautious yowls. Mrs Strickham frowned, glancing at them and then at the stone.

"Yes," she said to the foxes. "I'm quite all right."

One by one they rubbed their bodies against her. Caw couldn't work out what had just happened. He crouched down to take the stone.

"Don't!" said Mrs Strickham.

Caw paused, as she took a handkerchief out of her pocket. She stooped and picked up the stone in the cloth, more carefully this time, then closely inspected its surface.

"What is it?" said Crumb.

"I'm not at all sure," said Mrs Strickham. "Only that when I touched it, something didn't feel right."

"What kind of 'not right'?" asked Lydia.

Mrs Strickham glanced at Caw. "You've touched it too. Has it affected you?"

Caw started to shake his head, but Shimmer interrupted.

Actually, you have been a bit weird since you got it.

"In what way?" asked Caw.

Well... sort of distant, she said.

"Have I?"

We weren't going to say anything, added Glum. *Sometimes you don't seem to be listening. We told ourselves you had a lot to think about, but maybe it's got something to do with that stone.*

I don't like the look of it, added Screech.

"Quaker said it was dangerous," said Caw. "I think he knew that the Mother of Flies wanted it."

"The question is, why," said Mrs Strickham, gazing at the stone. "Caw, think! Is there anything else you can tell us?"

"The crows just told me I've not been myself since I got it," he said. "And actually..." He suddenly remembered the previous night, lying on Lydia's bedroom floor, and the sudden rush of despair as he touched the stone – the feeling that the crows might have left him. Could that have been the stone's doing as well?

"Actually what?" said Mrs Strickham.

"It's just, well..." Caw didn't know how to put it. "Perhaps it somehow takes away your link with your animals. I tried to turn into a crow when I went to see Quaker, and it didn't work. And sometimes I don't hear what the crows are saying any more. Just when I'm touching it."

"Well, it looks like a lump of rock to me," said Crumb. "I say we give it to that wretched fly talker and have done with it."

"You can't!" said Caw. Before he'd even thought about it, he reached out and snatched the stone back, handkerchief and all.

"Oh, can't we?" said Crumb. "She's got Pip, Caw. Doesn't that mean anything to you?"

"Yes, but..."

Crumb turned away with a snort of irritation. "Haven't you caused enough problems?" he said.

"I agree with Caw," said Mrs Strickham.

Crumb rounded on them both. "What? Pip's seven years old!"

"We can't afford to be emotional about this," said Lydia's mother.

Crumb scoffed, and pointed at Lydia. "And if they had her? What would you say then?"

Mrs Strickham took a deep breath, staring at her daughter. "Then I would find it very hard. But listen, Crumb. I think Caw might be on to something. The Mother of Flies has the good ferals. If this stone does what Caw suggests, she could use it to take away their powers. Then no one could stop her taking over the city."

"Sounds like a wild guess to me," said Crumb.

"Touch it then," said Lydia quickly. "Go on – if you're so sure it can't harm you."

"All right, then," said Crumb. He stepped confidently towards Caw, reaching out for the stone. But when his fingers were a few centimetres away, he stopped. The pigeons above were flapping wildly and one or two swooped low over his head. He drew back his hand, licking his lips nervously.

"Think about it," said Mrs Strickham. "Whatever that stone is – whatever it *does* – it's more precious to the Mother of Flies than the lives of all her enemies combined. It's brought her back to Blackstone. We can't afford to let her have it."

Caw remained silent as the fox feral and pigeon feral glared at one another. It was Crumb who looked away first. "All right, then. What's the plan?"

"I don't know," said Mrs Strickham. "But I might have an idea." She took her phone out of her pocket and stared at it, as though looking for an answer.

Lydia gently touched Screech's wing. "The wound looks clean, but you'll have a scar."

Screech nodded his beak proudly. *Roguish, some would say, eh, Shimmer?*

I see flirting with death hasn't made you any more modest, said Glum.

I'm just glad you're alive, said Shimmer.

"Your leg is broken too," said Lydia. Caw could see the kink in the delicate limb. "I should be able to splint it. Crumb, do you have any pieces of kindling, and some twine?"

"Upstairs," said the pigeon talker. "I'll get them." He still looked angry as he stalked off.

As they waited, Glum landed on Caw's shoulder.

You did the right thing, you know – telling them.

Caw nodded. Now he had revealed the secret, he wondered why he'd kept it so long. These were his friends, after all. Surely his mother wouldn't want him to keep secrets from them? He looked at the stone, lying in the handkerchief. Could it be true that it had the power to leach ferals of their gift?

He wrapped it up carefully and slipped it away, taking care not to touch it.

Crumb soon returned, carrying a small bundle. "These should do the trick," he said, handing them to Lydia. As she went to work, Mrs Strickham seemed to come to a decision.

"I think it's time I came clean," she muttered, clutching the phone with both hands.

Lydia frowned. "What do you mean?"

"If we need to get into Blackstone Prison, there's someone we both know who can help."

Lydia's eyes widened. "Dad!"

Mrs Strickham nodded slowly. "Blackstone prison's

a fortress," she said. "And he knows the place better than anyone."

"Can we trust him?" said Crumb. Mrs Strickham gave him a withering look, but Caw understood where Crumb was coming from. "Well, he's not one of us," Crumb added.

"Neither am I!" said Lydia. She stood up beside Screech. "There, that should do nicely."

Screech hopped upright. *Good as new*, he said.

A pigeon swooped down, landing on Crumb's hand. It cooed at him, and the pigeon feral's lips curled in a grim smile. "Thank you, Whitetail," he said.

"Care to share?" said Mrs Strickham.

"Well, I might have something that works in our favour. When I went upstairs, I wasn't just moping, you know."

"We're all in need of some good news, I think," said Lydia's mother.

Crumb's gaze lifted skyward. "And here it comes."

A large shape came flailing through the hole in the roof, carried by dozens of pigeons.

As the birds descended, they dropped a figure in a heap on the ground.

It was Selina Davenport.

Chapter 8

She looked utterly terrified, scrambling up as Mrs Strickham ran forward, gripped her by the neck and lifted her into the air. Foxes gathered and snarled from every side.

"Stop!" cried Caw.

"Mum!" said Lydia.

Selina's face was white with fear.

"Tell me why I shouldn't let my foxes tear your throat out?" hissed Lydia's mother.

Caw grabbed Mrs Strickham's arm and squeezed firmly. "Don't," he said. "Put her down so we can talk to her."

Mrs Strickham held on for a moment longer, then let go. Selina sank to the ground again, rubbing her neck. "I didn't mean... I didn't know..." she said.

Caw looked on her with contempt. "Being in my house?" he said. "That was all a trick, wasn't it?"

She looked up at him through tear-streaked eyes.

"I wanted to help you!" he snapped. "You betrayed me!"

"What do you expect? Her mother is the fly talker," said Crumb. "She's rotten to the core."

"What are you talking about?" mumbled Selina. "My mum's just in charge of the police."

"Don't play the fool with us," said Mrs Strickham.

Selina threw a desperate glance at Caw. "My mum told me there was a gang committing robberies in Blackstone. She said they moved around and they were impossible to catch. I just wanted to help."

Crumb scoffed. "She's lying. You expect us to believe that you've lived with the Mother of Flies your whole life and you didn't know?"

"I don't know what you're talking about," she said. "My mum's normal. She's not one of you lot. She can't talk to animals."

"Oh, *please!*" said Crumb, his face twisted. He waved a hand and the pigeons fell on Selina again. She kicked and screamed as they hoisted her back into the air.

"Let me go!" she demanded. "Why would I lie?"

Crumb lifted his arm and the pigeons carried Selina higher and higher.

"What are you doing?" said Caw nervously.

Crumb didn't take his eyes off Selina as he shouted over her cries. "You never met the eagle feral, did you?

He fought on the side of the Spinning Man in the Dark Summer. We were all terrified of him. His birds would sweep in from nowhere and snatch up their victims. His thing was to drop his enemies from a great height. Horrible way to die."

"Just do it then!" Selina shouted back at him. "If you want to think I'm that person, then I can't stop you. But I won't beg."

He's gone loco! said Screech.

"Crumb, no!" shouted Caw. "What if she's telling the truth?"

"I'll take that risk," said Crumb. He stepped forward, mouth set in a snarl and arms outstretched as the pigeons lifted Selina through the hole in the roof and out of sight. Caw saw Lydia's eyes widen in fear.

Quickly he summoned his crows. Glum, Screech and Shimmer flapped up. Others, more distant, just grey shapes in his mind, stirred as well. Caw knew they'd never arrive in time.

Crumb's fierce expression didn't waver. Then, as if he was scrunching paper into a ball, he clenched both fists and dropped his arms to his sides. A few seconds later the pigeons flew back in through the hole. Without Selina.

Caw stared, open-mouthed. Lydia let out a small wail of horror.

"What have you done with her?" said Mrs Strickham.

Crumb looked at each of them in turn, his eyes cold.

"Don't worry – they put her in the bell tower. The stairs collapsed long ago. She's stuck there until we decide what to do with her."

Lydia breathed out a long sigh. "You were just bluffing!"

Crumb brushed his hands together. "I know. I deserve an Oscar, right?"

Caw frowned. "What's an Oscar?"

"Never mind," said Crumb. "The point is, until I know we can trust her, she's staying up there."

I wouldn't bank on that, thought Caw, remembering how agile Selina had been on their roof-top escapade. "Do you think the Mother of Flies will do a deal?" he asked. "Her daughter in exchange for the ferals?"

"I don't trust either of them," said Mrs Strickham. "I say we try and free the ferals ourselves."

"With Dad's help?" asked Lydia.

Mrs Strickham nodded. "I've kept this secret for twenty years. This is not going to be easy."

With a sigh, she started to dial.

Caw was glad to be outside the church in the fresh air. He sat on a rusting metal bench tossing fragments of biscuit to a gathering of Crumb's pigeons.

Daft birds, aren't they? said Glum, perched behind him.

Barely a brain cell between them, said Shimmer, from the arm of the bench.

Are those cookies? said Screech from his shoulder. *You've got a hungry wounded warrior here.*

Caw fed Screech from his hand. He kept looking towards the church door, hoping Lydia would come out. He felt he needed to explain again, to make her understand why he hadn't shared the truth from the start. Because Felix Quaker told him to keep it safe? Because of something his mother had said in a dream?

He wished he'd never laid eyes on the stone. And if he hadn't gone to his house that night, he wouldn't have. He'd brought this all on himself, and now those closest to him were suffering too – all because he couldn't leave the past alone.

And because the past wouldn't leave him alone.

Everyone was blaming him, but it wasn't *all* his fault. He didn't ask for this life; to be abandoned, to be brought up eating worms in a nest, almost freezing to death every winter. He didn't ask to carry the blood of the crow line, or to guard a stupid evil stone!

He didn't want the burden. Or the honour. Or whatever it was supposed to be.

Hey, if you're just going to crush those things... said Screech.

Caw looked down and realised his fists were clenched around the packet of biscuits.

"Sorry," he said. He stood up quickly, sprinkling the remains in front of the bench. More pigeons flocked down.

Looks like our friend is making a break for it, said Glum.

Caw glanced up and saw Selina had swung her legs through the open section of the bell tower. She clung to the crumbling masonry.

And I thought pigeons were stupid, said Shimmer.

"I'd better stop her," said Caw. He took a deep breath, calling his birds to him.

Two minutes later, he hung in the grip of a murder of crows, hovering in the air beside Selina.

"Go back inside," he said. "You'll get yourself killed."

"What do you care?" she said. Her foot slipped a little, but she managed to cling on. A firm breeze ruffled her clothes. For a moment, Caw wasn't sure he *did* care.

"If you fall, Crumb will make me clean up the mess," he said.

Selina looked at him with her brow creased.

"It was a joke," he said. "Please, go back in. I want to talk to you."

A tile dislodged near her foot and rattled down the roof. Without a word, Selina scrambled back over the parapet and into the bell tower. Caw's crows set him down on the ledge and took flight with a fluttering of wings. All but his three faithful birds. The bell had disappeared long ago and all that remained were a few frayed sections of rope hanging from some sort of metal scaffold.

Selina sat against the wall inside, elbows on her knees and head bowed.

"OK," she said. "Let's talk."

I don't trust her one bit, said Shimmer.

Makes two of us, added Screech.

She'll try to trick you, said Glum.

Caw wished Milky were with him. He'd know exactly what to make of Selina Davenport. He waved the others off with his hand. "Give me a minute alone, will you?"

The three crows leapt from the tower and glided towards the ground.

Selina laughed harshly. "You have no idea how weird that looks," she said. "I mean – there's a woman who talks to ducks by the canal. Is she a feral too?"

Caw shrugged. "Maybe. She might just be crazy though."

Selina face twisted and, for a moment, he thought she was going to cry. But she didn't.

"You have every reason to hate me," she said.

"I know."

"I mean, *I'd* want to throw me off the church roof, if I were you."

Caw sat down opposite her. Shielded by the wall of the tower, the wind dropped completely.

"Let me ask you a question," he said. "Did you really not know your mum was a feral?"

Selina looked directly at him. "Cross my heart," she said.

Caw studied her face, looking for any twitch – any signal or clue that she might be lying. But what was the point? She'd lied before, constantly, and he hadn't sensed even the slightest untruth. If this was all a façade – if she was still just bluffing – he had no way of knowing.

Then he remembered – Mr Strickham didn't know about his wife and they were *married*. Maybe the Davenport family was just the same?

"But –" Selina paused – "I guess I knew she wasn't *totally* normal. We're not exactly close, you know? Not like my friends and their parents. I've always wished she'd spend more time with me, but she works crazy long hours. These last few years I've seen more of the cleaner than her."

Another thought occurred to Caw. If she was working for her mother still, did she know about the stone? He chose his next words carefully.

"Do you have any idea what she wants?" he asked.

Selina shook her head. "All she said was that you were dangerous, and that she needed some help because the police were drawing blanks. My job was to make friends with you. She sent me to your house weeks ago and told me to report in if you showed up. She wanted me to find out where you lived now." Selina sighed. "I really wanted to help her. But she wouldn't trust me to do anything else."

"You mean you offered?"

Selina's cheeks went crimson. "It was before I met you. I didn't know what you were like. But I could see straight away you weren't a criminal. God, you didn't even want to steal a packet of biscuits! In the end I didn't tell her. I wanted to find out more about you first. I don't know how those horrible people found us on the boat, and I don't know how she knew we'd be at the zoo."

Caw let her words sink in, testing her claims against his memory. Could she really be just a pawn in her mother's game?

"Her flies must have been watching you," he said. "Watching us. Those people in the zoo were innocent. You saw them – children and old people, mostly."

"I know that," Selina said. "But I had no idea the police would show up." Her eyes flashed with the old defiance. "You guys took *me* there, remember. That fox lady wouldn't have let me go even if I'd wanted to..."

Crumb's voice interrupted them. "Don't let her hear you calling her that," he said. The pigeon feral appeared silhouetted against the sky above them, held aloft by pigeons. "Come on, if we're going to break into Blackstone Prison, we need to make a plan."

"What about me?" said Selina.

"You, my girl, are coming too," said Crumb, with a grim smile.

Chapter 9

"**S**he is not coming with us!" said Lydia, when they were all back on the ground. "Are you mad? She'll give us away at the first opportunity."

"No, she won't," said Mrs Strickham, glaring at Selina. "Because if she does, my foxes will make her pay. Understand?"

Selina nodded, her face white.

"Don't tell me you agree with all this?" Lydia asked Caw.

Caw didn't know what to say.

"I might be able to talk to my mum," Selina said. "Make her see sense."

"You won't say a word," said Mrs Strickham. "I'll be keeping an eye on you. When all this is over, then we'll decide what to do with you."

Lydia didn't look at Caw as they climbed into the car. She was obviously still fuming as they drove off into the dark roads of Blackstone. "I'm sorry," Caw murmured to her. "I should have told you about the stone." But she ignored him.

A few streets away from the prison, Mrs Strickham pulled over in an alley and killed the lights. A shadow detached from a wall. It was Mr Strickham, dressed in jeans and a black sweater. His skin was pale.

"Stay inside a moment," said Mrs Strickham. She cracked open the door and climbed out. Caw watched her silently approach her husband. They stopped when they were a couple of metres apart and didn't move any closer. From the corner of his eye, Caw saw Lydia leaning forward.

He couldn't tell who spoke first, but he saw Mr Strickham shaking his head, then gesticulating angrily. Lydia's mother held her ground, her body language giving nothing away as her lips moved. She looked completely calm. At one point Mr Strickham stabbed a finger towards the car, then he paced over and flung open the door. "Lydia, out!" he said.

Lydia did as she was told.

"Dad, please," she said.

"No!" he answered. "This is ridiculous. I don't know what sort of game you two are playing, but it's gone far enough."

"It's not a game, sir," said Crumb, unfolding his limbs from the car. Caw got out the other side, while Selina remained in the back.

"So," said Mr Strickham, glancing at each of them. "You're all *ferals* too, I suppose? You can *communicate* –" he used quote marks with his hands – "with animals?"

Crumb clicked his fingers and a bank of a dozen pigeons swooped and landed on the roof of the car. Glum and Screech landed on Caw's shoulders without even being asked.

Caw couldn't read the emotions shifting across Mr Strickham's face. After several seconds, he looked at Lydia first, then his wife. Several foxes had gathered silently at her feet.

"I'm just glad you came, Tony," she said.

Lydia's father exhaled a long breath, seemed to be about to speak, then paused. "It can't... it can't be true."

"It is," said Lydia. She reached for her father's hand. "We wouldn't lie to you, Dad."

"But you did," he said sadly. He pulled Lydia into an embrace and stared over her head at his wife. "You lied to me for years."

For a few moments, no one spoke.

It was Crumb who broke the silence. "So can you get us in or not?" he asked.

Mr Strickham stiffened.

"Dad?" asked Lydia, breaking their hug.

He looked down at her. "I don't like it," he said. "What you're doing is against the law. You're nothing better than vigilantes, really, and if you weren't my family, I'd be tempted to call the federal authorities. It's not too late to reconsider, you know?"

Mrs Strickham shook her head briskly. "We need you, Tony. Are you with us, or not?"

"I suppose I have no choice," he said. "But I can't get you in through the front door. We'll have to go another way."

Caw listened as Lydia's father laid out the plan. He might not officially work at the prison any more, but the guards still knew him. He'd march right up to the front gates. He thought he might be able to claim he was collecting the last of his belongings from his office.

Meanwhile Caw and the others would enter through the sewer tunnels, the same way that the disciples of the Spinning Man had escaped a few weeks before. Mr Strickham was sure repairs hadn't started on the breakout tunnel yet. "The City Council keep promising the funds, but then they always do," he said.

"Good luck," said Mrs Strickham. She reached out to touch her husband, but he backed away. Lydia hugged him fiercely.

"Be careful, Dad. Any sign of trouble, you run."

"Same goes for you," he said. Then he strode off into the night.

Caw knew that his words of warning would be ignored. No one was backing down tonight.

Already several foxes had begun to emerge from the surrounding streets, padding silently towards them, and pigeons were settling on the rooftops above.

"Ready?" said Crumb, holding Selina by the arm.

Mrs Strickham took a crowbar and a torch from the boot of the car and went to the manhole cover in the alleyway. It was loose and she prised it open in a matter of seconds. Her foxes went down first, disappearing into the dark hole. Lydia followed, then Selina.

As Crumb went down, Caw made a decision and summoned his crows. Shimmer, Screech and Glum landed beside him.

Caw took the stone from his pocket and placed it between them, keeping hold of the handkerchief. "Take this to the old bandstand in the park," he whispered. "Bury it under the bench."

Why? said Glum.

"I don't want to risk the Mother of Flies getting it," he said. "And if I don't come out again..."

Don't talk like that, said Shimmer.

"... take it somewhere far away," he finished.

Crumb stuck his head out again and Caw positioned his body to hide the stone. "What are you waiting for?" he said.

"Nothing," said Caw.

As Crumb lowered his body again, Caw followed.

See you soon, said Screech, hopping on to the stone and clutching it in a talon. *Good luck!*

Caw gave them a wave and descended the ladder, then pulled the manhole cover over him with an echoing clang.

An arc of torchlight illuminated the narrow tunnel. Caw could see a channel of foul-smelling slime sitting stagnant to the depth of about an inch. Mrs Strickham's foxes kept their paws well out of it and Caw placed his feet on either side. He had to stand in a slight crouch.

Lydia held the rough map her father had drawn.

They trooped along the tunnel, stopping at intersections to check the way. There was no life down here, and the only sounds were their breathing and the shuffle of footsteps. Caw began to feel closed in and doubts crept into his mind. What if Mr Strickham had got the route wrong? Would they even be able to find their way back?

The foxes' eyes gleamed like gold coins in the torchlight.

"This should be it," said Lydia, pausing at the side of the tunnel. Caw saw a shaft leading off the main conduit at chest height, barely wide enough to crawl down. The metal cladding was discoloured with streaks of orange and green.

"I'll go first," said Caw.

As he reached up, Lydia caught his arm. "What you

said in the car," she said. "About the stone. I just want you to know that I... well, I understand why you kept it secret."

Caw was so grateful he didn't know what to say. He smiled in the darkness. Then he pulled himself into the shaft, edging along on his hands and knees, with the torch shaking in his hand.

The shaft followed a slight incline for several metres, then reached what looked like a dead end. But on closer inspection, he saw it turned vertically upwards. He manoeuvred himself around the bend, wondering how on earth a man of Jawbone's size could have managed. The dog feral had been well over six feet tall and thick with muscle. Caw saw the glint of a metal grate above, and light beyond. He reached up. The grate moved easily in his hand and he pushed it carefully aside. Still, the scrape of metal seemed horribly loud.

He held his breath, expecting to hear guards' whistles or alarms.

Nothing.

"Go on then," said Crumb from below. "I can't stand this stink any more."

Caw stretched up with both hands, grabbing the cold floor.

Fingers closed around his wrist and he let out a cry.

"Quiet!" said Mr Strickham, leaning over the hole.

Caw's thumping heart subsided and he let Lydia's

father heave him up. He emerged into a shower room of grubby tiles.

"Sorry if I scared you," said Mr Strickham.

Together, they helped the others from the drainage shaft. Lydia brushed down her clothes. "*That* was horrible," she said.

"Getting in was easier than I expected," said Mr Strickham.

"We still need to be careful," said his wife. "Cynthia Davenport will have eyes everywhere." Mrs Strickham alone looked unperturbed by the expedition through the claustrophobic sewers. Her black coat didn't even seem dirty, whereas Crumb was caked in all sorts of scuffs and stains.

"There's another problem," said Mr Strickham. "I've already checked the systems and the prisoners haven't been logged. That means I don't know which cells they're being held in."

"Where are the high security areas?" said Caw.

"There are several," said Mr Strickham, "all spread about the prison. That way, security breaches can be contained more easily."

Something scurried across the tiles, making Lydia jump. One of Mrs Strickham's foxes pounced and landed on top of it.

"Off," she said, and the fox lifted its front paws. It was a cockroach.

"We always tried to keep the place clean, but we never could get rid of the damn things," said Mr Strickham. His gaze was fixed on the fox that his wife had controlled, as effortlessly as though it were part of her own body.

Caw caught Lydia's eye. A cockroach might mean something – a face from the past he had hoped never to see again. He leant down. "Take us to your master," he said.

Mr Strickham glared at him. "So now you're going to tell me that insects speak human?" he said.

"This one might," said Lydia.

The roach scurried away, Caw and the others following close behind. It moved quickly, never seeming to doubt where it was going, and they had to jog to keep up. They climbed up metal stairs, along corridors, past featureless, identical cell doors. The whole place smelled of disinfectant, but other odours lurked beneath – stale sweat and desperation. Soon the signs on the wall read 'B-WING'. The roach slipped under a barred doorway.

"This is one of the high security areas," said Mr Strickham, sliding an access card through a reader and cranking open the door. "But I'm pretty sure all these cells are empty."

The roach disappeared under a door labelled "Cell B23".

The door was solid steel with a grille as big as a

letterbox at head height. Before Caw even put his eye to it, he had guessed what he'd see.

"Hello, crow talker," said a voice from the dark room. Caw pressed a switch beside the door, and a light came on inside. A doughy face with a stubbled chin leered at him, eyes set in hollow sockets. Caw's heart skipped a beat, but he didn't look away. He wasn't the same scared boy who would have run before.

"Hello, Scuttle," he said.

Chapter 10

The cockroach feral sat hunched on a thick mattress, dressed in an orange prison jumpsuit just like the one he'd been wearing when Caw first encountered him breaking out of prison many weeks before. Caw saw that his face was mottled with bruises and there was a cut above his eyebrow.

"Come to gloat, have you?" Scuttle said.

"Of course he hasn't," said a woman from the cell opposite. Selina jumped as Mamba's darting black eyes appeared at the grille. "Let me guess, crow talker – you want to know about the Mother of Flies? Ah, and if it isn't young Lydia Strickham as well. Tell me, got a new dog yet?"

Lydia rushed at the door, pounding with her fists. "I hope you rot in there!"

Mrs Strickham tugged her back and stepped in front

of Mamba's cell, her foxes pawing at the door. "What do you know about her, snake talker?"

"Nothing," hissed Mamba, retreating from the door. "Don't tell them anything, Scuttle."

Caw looked back in at the cockroach feral. Only one person would be daring enough to beat up a feral who controlled cockroaches. "She did that to you, didn't she?" he said. "Cynthia Davenport."

"What?" said Selina. "What did she do?" She pushed alongside Caw and looked into the cell. Her mouth opened in a small gasp.

Scuttle's hands went up to his bruised face, as if remembering the blows.

"I don't believe it," breathed Selina.

"She never liked the Spinning Man," he said. "She took it out on me."

"Scuttle, shut up!" snapped Mamba from the cell opposite. She sounded angry, but scared too.

"Open the door," said Mrs Strickham. "I can make him talk."

Mr Strickham slid a key card down the sensor on the right of the door. Caw heard bolts slide across and the door opened of its own accord.

Scuttle pressed himself further into the corner of the cell. As Caw and the others entered, several roaches scurried across the floor and darted inside Scuttle's clothes. "You can't hurt me any more than she did," said the hunched feral.

"Are you sure?" said Mrs Strickham, prowling forwards with her foxes.

One roach was slower than the others and ran in panicked circles. Crumb trapped it beneath his foot and the insect screeched.

"Stop that!" said Scuttle. "It hurts him!"

Crumb sneered, and pressed his weight harder on the shell. "They say cockroaches would be the only thing to survive a nuclear war. Think this one can survive my size tens?"

"All right! All right!" said Scuttle. "I'll tell you all I know, but it's not much. The Mother of Flies is up to something in the prison."

Mamba's door shook. "Don't tell them, you wretch. She'll know!"

"Keep talking," said Crumb.

"She's been moving the prisoners around," said Scuttle. "The most dangerous ones. She's transferred them somewhere. D-wing is totally empty now."

So she can lock up the ferals there, thought Caw. He looked at Mrs Strickham, who gave him a nod. No doubt she was thinking the same thing.

"It's something to do with him!" said Scuttle, pointing a stubby finger at Caw.

Caw shivered. "Me?"

"That's why she did this to me," said Scuttle. "She wanted to know everything about him. Where he lived. Where he went."

"And what did you tell him?" asked Caw.

The roach feral shrugged. "What we knew, which wasn't much. We told her where your parents lived."

Caw looked at Selina. "So that's how you knew where to find me?"

"She just gave me an address," Selina pleaded. "I didn't know where it came from."

Mamba smiled, her teeth sparkling. "You won't defeat her. You know that, don't you?"

"No one cares what you think," said Lydia.

Mamba ignored her. "The Mother of Flies isn't like the Spinning Man," she said. "She might come from a wretched line, but she's cruel, powerful and devious. She wouldn't join us in the Dark Summer – she always had bigger plans."

Caw wondered if the crows had managed to hide the stone. They'd be careful, of course, but what if a fly was watching them?

"We're finished here," said Mrs Strickham. "Let's go."

Scuttle jumped up, wringing his hands. "Wait! Please! I can't stay in here! Maybe I can help you in some way. I could be your spy?"

Crumb lifted his boot and let the cockroach scurry back to his master. Then he slammed the cell door. "You're right where you belong."

"Both of you," hissed Lydia at Mamba.

"I'd rather be in a cell than suffer what the Mother of Flies will do to you," said Mamba.

Caw watched her darkly shining eyes shrink away from the grille.

Mrs Strickham beckoned for Caw and the others to follow her and they set off back the way they'd come.

"Don't leave me!" cried Scuttle. "I'm begging you!"

Caw felt a shred of sympathy for the cockroach feral in spite of everything. But by the time they'd turned a few corners, his voice had died away.

"Where's D-wing?" asked Crumb. "That's where she must have taken the ferals."

"Follow me," said Lydia's father.

They pressed on, slowly, through the abandoned passages, past empty cells and bare scuffed walls of peeling paint. Foxes trailed after them. Caw had lost his bearings completely, but Mr Strickham seemed sure of himself.

"She'll have the place guarded, won't she?" said Crumb.

"Yes, but we still have the trump card," said Mrs Strickham. She turned to look at Selina, her glare more fierce and deadly than anything Caw had seen before. Like a fox that's seen its prey, he thought. "Maybe we should see how much the Mother of Flies really loves her daughter."

"What?" said Selina, edging closer to Caw. "What are you going to do to me?"

"I don't think—" Crumb began.

"Quiet," said Mrs Strickham. "She's one life – the ferals are many."

Selina suddenly broke into a sprint. Immediately several foxes were on her heels. She screamed as one leapt up, snatching her jacket in its teeth. As she reached the corner of the corridor she flung herself against the wall just before the foxes finally pinned her down. A siren began to wail, deafeningly loud.

Caw realised what she'd done and his heart dropped.

"She's hit the emergency alarm," shouted Mr Strickham. "They'll be on us in less than a minute."

"Which way?" Crumb demanded.

Mr Strickham shook his head in panic. "I... I don't know."

Crumb grabbed him by the shoulder. "Where will the guards come from?"

Mr Strickham raised a trembling finger and pointed past Selina. "From there. No, wait..." He spun on his heels, eyes narrowing as his mind worked. "We need to head for the service entrance. Through the exercise yard. There's only a single guard this time of night."

They set off at a run, Mrs Strickham grabbing hold of Selina and dragging her with them.

Caw looked at Cynthia Davenport's daughter in shock. Just as he'd been starting to trust her. But it was Mrs

Strickham's fault too. She had threatened to kill her, after all...

At each door they reached, Mr Strickham used his card to get past. Caw's heart was thumping and he expected guards to appear at every turn. At the end of a corridor, Mr Strickham swiped and a door opened on to a bare concrete yard, surrounded on three sides by tall windowless walls and on the fourth by a double fence topped with razor wire, with a tall closed gate at the centre. Two guard towers stood overlooking the gate.

"This way," said Mr Strickham. "Follow me."

The foxes streaked into the yard first. Halfway across, Caw sensed the buzz of a fly beside his ear and was about to call out when bright lights blinded him. He skidded to a halt, shielding his eyes. When he opened them again, he realised that spotlights were blazing down from each corner of the yard. He saw silhouettes of guards on the walls, and more in the towers, all angling rifles on to Caw and his friends. The red dots of laser sights traced across the ground and over their bodies.

They were completely surrounded. Caw thought about reaching for the Crow's Beak on his back, but he knew he'd be dead before he could get the blade an inch from its harness.

He heard the hum of the electric gate opening, and then Cynthia Davenport walked casually through, still dressed in her black suit and flanked by Mr Silk and

Pinkerton. Both were wearing police uniforms. The gate closed behind them.

"Nice of you to join us, Mr Carmichael," she said, her breath misting the air. "And you've brought some friends, I see."

"Mum!" said Selina. "It was me who set off the alarm! Mum, they're saying things about you. I don't understand. They were going to hurt me."

Cynthia Davenport ignored her daughter, and kept her eyes on Caw. "Have you brought the stone?"

Caw clenched his jaw and shook his head. "You'll never have it."

"Oh, you silly, silly boy," said the Mother of Flies. "Why make it so hard?"

Caw saw Mrs Strickham move quickly to his left. She grabbed Selina, whipped her around and cupped one hand under her chin.

"Lower your guns, or I'll snap her neck!" she said.

The red dots didn't waver, and neither did Cynthia Davenport's expression. She looked at her daughter as if she were a piece of dirt.

"All I want is the Midnight Stone," she said.

"Mum?" said Selina. "But... she's crazy... she'll..."

"I'll do it, I swear!" said Mrs Strickham. She looked desperate, confused, like a cornered animal.

"If you think I can be bargained with, you're wrong," said the Mother of Flies.

Selina was staring at her mother, wild-eyed. "How can you say that?" she murmured. "Mum, please..."

Mrs Strickham held firm. "Don't test me, fly talker," she said.

Caw could see the determination in her face and it terrified him. She wasn't bluffing. But neither was the Mother of Flies.

"Arrest them all," said Cynthia Davenport. "Alive, preferably. Or dead, if it comes to it."

Caw jumped forward to tear Mrs Strickham away, and at the same time two foxes launched themselves at Cynthia Davenport. Several rifle shots cracked above and the foxes scampered clear. Selina broke free.

He wasn't sure what happened next, only that more bullets flew and a policeman fell screaming from above, hitting the ground with a thud. The pale shapes of pigeons fell from the sky, swooping to attack the other officers. Mr Strickham jumped in front of Lydia, shielding her with his body.

"Caw, get out of here!" yelled Lydia. "Use your crows!"

Caw heard pigeons screeching, and looked up. Each one was thrashing, its feathers covered in a black swarm of flies. He couldn't call his crows into this trap as well.

Police were coming through the gates now, surrounding Crumb and Mr Strickham. "I can't believe this is happening," Mr Strickham muttered, his face deathly pale.

"On the ground!" said one of the cops, pointing his gun at Caw.

Caw backed away, looking for an escape route. Red dots danced across his chest.

The fence was too high and the gate was blocked. There was no way out.

Except one.

"Get down, kid!" shouted another officer.

Caw closed his eyes. *Come on!* his mind screamed. *Change!*

He remembered the first time it had happened – how he'd managed to lose himself, to release his body from its human form. But that was before he'd touched the Midnight Stone. What if it had weakened him permanently?

"Last chance. Lie down, or we'll fire!"

Caw ignored the waves of fear smashing through him. He lowered himself to his knees. He felt his body lighten and the shouts of the prison yard become more distant.

It's happening...

His limbs seemed to turn to liquid, his bones shifting horribly, tendons stretching to breaking point. He cried out in pain, opening his eyes to see the faces of the police aghast. They lowered their guns, slowly, in horror. Only one fired, but Caw felt the bullet whizz past his shoulder.

He fell forward and tried to catch himself but his arms had gone and instead his feet left the ground. He flailed, and again he rose. He saw his wings on either side and flapped them more forcefully until at last they lifted him right above the police officers' heads. He soared higher and higher – marvelling at the power of his crow body.

A cloud of moths came to intercept him, screeching, but with a flick of his wings he slid beneath them. He felt them land across his back with soft, insistent thumps. Caw thrashed and snapped his beak, but he couldn't fight them off. He couldn't even see for all the wings.

He tried to think above the panic to survive. He cast out his summons with the power of his mind and saw them coming. A dozen crows. They swept past, gathering up the moths in their beaks and talons, crushing their bodies and hurling them down. The weight on Caw's back was gone and he righted himself, climbing higher. The moths pursued, a swathe of fluttering grey, but the crows regrouped and attacked, smashing their column to pieces.

Above the prison yard, Caw saw it all. Mr Strickham and Lydia being dragged to their feet and pulled away from each other. Mrs Strickham still fighting as officers piled on to her. Selina gazing open-mouthed to one side, her body slack, pressed up against a wall with her hands cuffed behind her back. She looked neither afraid nor defiant, just... lost.

Cynthia Davenport had gone. He turned his head, sweeping his crow gaze over the vista.

No, there she was. Somehow, in just a matter of seconds, she had reached the top of one of the towers. She was standing there, watching him.

Rage boiled in Caw's chest, making his feathers tingle.

Attack! he willed.

The crows wheeled behind him and together they swooped towards her.

She watched him coming, a grin on her face, as if she didn't care at all.

Caw gathered his strength, turning up his talons to rake across her skin. She couldn't escape. And then, a split-second before impact, she seemed to dematerialise in front of him, exploding into a storm of black dots.

Flies!

Caw adjusted his flight to avoid smashing into the side of the tower and turned on the wing. The other crows did the same. Where Cynthia Davenport had been, now there was a swarm of flies, so dense in places they were a solid mass. They shot towards him, coating his wings, and their buzzing burrowed into his ears and made him want to clamp his eyes shut.

Caw tried to shake them loose and fly away, but each time he threw them off, they simply fell on him again in a raucous assault. He tried to call his other crows, but couldn't focus. He felt the sting of a hundred bites across his body and sensed her hatred in each one. He flapped madly, and broke free.

Caw shot across the rooftops, trying to escape. The flies pursued on every side, sometimes swarming ahead, sometimes dropping back.

They're playing with me! Like it's a game.

By the time he reached the railway line, he was tiring, but the flies were relentless. He dipped and swooped under a bridge, hoping to lose them, but on the other side they were waiting, hovering. A mass slammed into one wing, tipping him over. Caw lost his bearings and couldn't stop as the rails rushed towards him.

He slammed into tracks and, for a moment, all he felt was breathless pain. He bounced and slid, and when he fetched up at the side of the lines, he saw his leg bleeding through his torn trousers. He was a human again.

Caw rolled over – his hands were scraped and bloody, and his shoulder felt all wrong. When he tried to move it, the bones ground against each other, making his vision blur. The wave of agony brought bile into his throat.

The flies descended in a black cloud, then a foot above the ground they coalesced into the shape of Cynthia Davenport. Her feet touched down smoothly. Taking out her phone, she muttered a few words into it, then strode towards him.

"Not your best landing, I would have thought," she said. Leaning down, she grabbed his foot and began to tug him across the metal rails and into the middle of the line. Caw had no strength to fight her, and his shoulder screamed.

She let him drop, and placed a dagger-like heel in the middle of his chest, pushing him back to the ground.

"You might be able to turn into one animal, but you see, I can turn into thousands," she said. "Now, where is the Midnight Stone?"

Caw tried to move, but he was too weak.

The Mother of Flies pressed more weight on to him, the point of her heel right over his heart.

"Where is it?" she said again.

The ground began to tremble beneath them. Craning his neck, Caw saw two wide headlights approaching along the tracks.

"Where is the stone, crow talker?" she shouted. It was the first time Caw had heard her raise her voice. He squirmed uselessly. He couldn't escape, but he couldn't tell her either. He couldn't let his mother down. Over her shoulder, he saw his three crow companions circling. He willed them to stay back.

"You'll never have it," he said.

The glare of the lights lit up Cynthia Davenport's face as the train horn sounded.

"So be it," she said.

Caw heard the piercing screech of brakes, but it was far too late to escape. He closed his eyes, ready to die.

Chapter 11

The roar of the train seemed to burrow into his head and the air filled with the smell of engine oil, heat and dust.

Caw felt his body jerked aside and pain shot through his shoulder again. It took a moment to realise he wasn't dead. The Mother of Flies had pulled him upright and gripped him tight by the collar as the train thundered past just a foot away, shaking his bones. Then it was gone, carrying its sound and fury off into the night and leaving the air trembling in its wake. Caw felt barely strong enough to stand.

"Brave," she said. "But this is a waste of time. You're only delaying the inevitable."

A limo pulled up on the road below the bridge. From its huge grille and bulk, Caw guessed it was armoured. One of the rear doors opened and Mr Silk climbed out. He'd changed out of the police uniform back into his white hat and suit, which was covered in the shimmering bodies of his moths.

Cynthia Davenport spun Caw round and then dissolved into flies. They swarmed over his skin and suddenly the world lurched as he felt himself hoisted into the air by the buzzing bodies. The sensation was weird and frightening – and completely unlike when the crows carried him. He was a prisoner.

The swarm lowered him on to the ground beside the limo, then dispersed, flying up and away. Caw felt cold metal clasp over his wrists as a pair of handcuffs clicked into place. The pain from his shoulder brought him close to retching as the moth feral shoved him into the car. He fell awkwardly across the seats. Mr and Mrs Strickham and Lydia sat opposite, all in cuffs like Caw. Mrs Strickham's eyes passed over him emptily.

"Do make yourself comfortable," said Mr Silk with a smile. He slammed the door.

"Caw, are you OK?" said Lydia, eyes fixed on his torn clothes.

Caw righted himself, hissing through his teeth as his bones ground together. "I think my shoulder is dislocated," he said. "Where's Crumb?"

"They kept him at the prison," said Mr Strickham. His cheek was badly grazed, his lip swollen, and he looked utterly dejected.

The limo started to move. Still Mrs Strickham only stared into space.

"And... Selina?" asked Caw.

"Why d'you even care?" snapped Lydia. "She betrayed us again, the first chance she got."

It was true. But Caw knew what he'd seen in her face in the prison yard – the look of fear as she struggled to understand, of being completely lost. And he knew how that felt.

The car drove fast, throwing them around in the back every time it swerved. Caw glanced out of the window. They were heading south, unless he was mistaken, and back towards the river. The prison was in the other direction entirely. *Where's she taking us?*

"So where is this stone that she's after?" asked Mr Strickham.

Caw checked all around for flies before he answered. "I hid it."

"Well, where?" asked Lydia's father angrily.

"Don't tell us," said Mrs Strickham. "It's better that way."

Mr Strickham rolled his eyes. "For god's sake! This is crazy. If it's this stone she wants, then why the hell don't we—"

"Please, Dad, don't," said Lydia. "Don't you see, Caw was right. This whole thing – Selina being at Caw's house, the raid at the zoo, the prison – the Mother of Flies planned it all. She wants that stone more than anything else. It's like Mamba said – she's been a step ahead from the start."

Mr Strickham's mouth moved as if he was about to say something else, but he fell silent.

After a few moments, the car stopped with the engine still running. Caw heard the sound of electric gates opening, then they rolled forward more slowly. Finally the engine died, and the door was flung open.

"Out," said Mr Silk, tapping his foot impatiently.

Caw went first, gingerly manoeuvring himself out of the door. The pain in his shoulder had dulled to a pulsing ache. He realised at once that they were in the financial district, surrounded by towers of steel and glass. It wasn't a place he'd often visited – there was nothing to scavenge here and most of the buildings had cameras or security guards. The car had pulled up in a wide forecourt decorated with potted plants and a sparkling fountain. It was completely silent, apart from the trickling of the water.

The front door on the other side of the car opened. Caw expected to see Cynthia Davenport, but instead it was the pale figure of her daughter who climbed out. Caw's heart twisted with a surge of emotion as she glanced up at him, her face puffy from crying.

"Get a move on," said Mr Silk.

Selina stood firm, looking up at the towering building. "What is this place?" she said.

"Your new home," said Mr Silk. "The concierge will tell you where to go." He shoved her in the back and she walked slowly towards the entrance.

"Traitor!" shouted Lydia.

Selina didn't even seem to hear as she went up the front steps and disappeared inside.

Pinkerton got out of the car next. Like Mr Silk, she had changed out of her police gear. Several squeaking rats poured after her as she went to join Mr Silk.

"I think we'd better go inside," said the moth feral. He took off his hat and bowed to Velma Strickham. "Ladies first."

Mrs Strickham didn't move.

"You can try to summon all the foxes you want, but trust me, there won't be many around here," said Mr Silk. "They lay down poison, you see, for pests." He tipped his hat. "Please," he pointed towards the lobby. "My manners have limits."

"Come on," said Mr Strickham. "Let's see what she has to say."

He led the way up the steps, his wife and daughter following. Caw came last, his arm gripped by Pinkerton, her rats scuttling around his feet.

"You sh-shouldn't have m-m-made her angry," said Pinkerton in Caw's ear.

As they walked through the door, Caw glanced back

and scanned the sky for his crows. Had they followed? If so, he couldn't see them.

Once inside, Mr Silk and Pinkerton escorted them across a marble floor, skirting the fountain. Selina had already disappeared. A doorman on a desk paid no attention to the strange crowd, or the rodents. Another of her employees, thought Caw. His blood was pumping. He had no idea what they were walking into.

At a bank of elevators, Mr Silk pushed a button and waited. "She won't let you take your rats up there," he said to Pinkerton.

"W-w-why not?" said the feral.

"Because, my dear, even the fly talker thinks they're vermin."

Pinkerton scowled.

The elevator door pinged open and they were all herded in. As the door closed on the rats, Caw saw that even though their wrists were cuffed behind their backs, Mr Strickham was still holding on to Lydia's hands with his own.

He doesn't know if we're getting out of this alive, thought Caw.

Caw watched the numbers light up as the elevator climbed smoothly. The walls were glass, and while the lobby dropped away on one side, through the rear pane Caw saw the city loom into view. The neighbouring skyscrapers were dark shadows against the sky, but further off lights twinkled across the river, and the glow of car headlamps threaded across the city. So many ordinary people, who had no idea what was going on beneath their noses.

At the seventieth floor, the elevator came to a stop and the doors opened.

Caw wasn't sure what he'd expected. An office, perhaps. But they stepped out on to a walkway overlooking a huge, open-plan apartment. Mrs Strickham was taking it all in as well, coolly surveying her surroundings. One side of the apartment was entirely glass, giving an incredible view of the city. Huge abstract paintings covered white walls and a fire burned in a free-standing hearth. Large leather sofas were arranged around a glass table on a rug made of some sort of animal skin. Off to the side, forming the short section of an L-shape, Caw caught a glimpse of what looked like a kitchen.

The place couldn't have been more different from the dilapidated sewing factory where the Spinning Man had based his operations. Everything was pure luxury – the sort of stuff most normal people craved.

But there was a smell that didn't fit at all. Something that made Caw's stomach turn.

They were led down a set of stairs from the walkway and across the lounge, towards a long dining table lined with chairs. Caw's heart jolted as he saw what lay there.

"Urgh!" said Lydia, suddenly halting and clapping her hands over her mouth and nose.

In the centre, half-decomposed and grinning up at them, was a pig's head. Flies crawled over its rotting surface and maggots squirmed from an empty eye socket. Mr Strickham wretched.

Pinkerton sniggered. "G-g-got to keep her babies happy."

Lydia's mother merely raised an eyebrow. "Just take us to her."

At the end of the dining table was a set of double doors, one open slightly. As they passed, Caw caught a glimpse of a low-lit carpeted room. Several men and women were drinking beer from bottles at a bar and playing pool. They were muttering to each other, and one or two noticed Caw and his companions, but none came out.

Mr Strickham stopped suddenly. "Hey!" he said. "I know you."

A particularly fierce-looking man with tattoos over his arms and a crooked mouth put down his beer bottle on the bar and stalked over, spinning a pool cue.

"You're Lugmann," said Mr Strickham. "You were in D-wing."

Lugmann grinned, squeezing his frame through the single open door. His mouth glinted with several silver teeth. "Not any more, Governor," he said. He raised the pool cue and Mr Strickham backed away. Mr Silk grabbed

Lugmann's arm, and Caw saw a tattoo of a fly on the inside of the convict's wrist.

"I wouldn't be trying that if I were you," said the moth feral. "Our mistress would not be happy."

Lugmann grunted and jutted out his chin. "When the time comes, Governor," he said. "And I assure you, it will come." He dragged a finger across his throat, turned and walked back to his game of pool.

"I think we know where all the high security inmates are now," muttered Mr Strickham, as they were pushed on. "In that room."

Caw frowned. Why would the Mother of Flies have human henchmen? Then he remembered what Mrs Strickham had said in the taxi on the way to the prison – how the fly ferals had always been looked down on by the other ferals. Perhaps the Mother of Flies had no choice but to make do with humans? And the only wretched ferals who would follow her – the moth feral and the rat feral. The lowest of the low.

As they passed the table with the pig's head, the flies all stopped moving. Caw shuddered. They were watching, he realised. Mr Silk led them to a single door set in an alcove. It looked completely out of place in the fancy apartment – solid metal, as if it belonged in a warehouse.

Mr Silk knocked, then waited a few moments, before touching a key card to a glowing red sensor at the side. It changed to green and the doors slid open. A blast of cool air rushed over them and Lydia gave a disgusted gasp.

Caw recoiled in horror from the nightmare scene in front of him. The room was full of meat. Suspended from the ceiling by metal hooks were several skinned carcasses, their marbled flesh giving off an iron tang. Caw pulled himself together as he realised they weren't human, but animals. They looked like pigs, sheep, and one that was surely a cow, split in two to reveal a huge ribcage laced with a layer of fat. All of them were headless.

"In," said Mr Silk.

Lydia jammed her foot against the doorway, but Pinkerton shoved her inside.

Though the floor was tiled black, the walls and ceiling were gleaming stainless steel with no windows and only a few small vents at ceiling height. As they passed the first few hanging corpses, Caw saw Cynthia Davenport sitting in the middle of the room on a simple metal stool, her black suit at odds with the butcher-shop surroundings.

"I'm sorry if you find this place distasteful," she said, her breath misting in the cold air, "but my children do have quite an appetite."

Mr Silk gave Caw a shove in the back, forcing him further into the room between the hanging carcasses of meat. Lydia shrank away to stop herself bashing into a sheep's corpse.

"You're disgusting!" she said.

The Mother of Flies smiled. "Welcome to the food chain," she replied.

Mrs Strickham moved in front of her daughter. "Don't talk to her," she snapped.

"You think I'm not good enough, fox feral?" said Cynthia Davenport, standing up. "Not worthy even to speak to your daughter?" She walked right up to Lydia's mother and raised a hand with long black-painted nails. "You always were an arrogant line. I bet you never thought the lowly fly feral would get the better of you, did you?" Velma Strickham didn't even flinch as Davenport trailed a long painted nail across her cheek. "Try anything silly and I promise there's room for a few foxes in here." Her eyes went to the ceiling hooks.

"What do you want?" said Mr Strickham.

The Mother of Flies ignored the question, her attention focused on the fox feral. "I've heard a lot about you. You killed the spider feral. The first time, anyway."

"When you were cowering in hiding," said Mrs Strickham. "While *real* ferals fought for this city."

Cynthia Davenport gave a high-pitched shriek of laughter. "The Dark Summer, you mean? A petty squabble in which I had nothing to gain or lose. No, I pick my battles, fox talker. He came to me, you know – the spider feral. Begged me to join him. He knew what I was capable of; he saw what the fly line had become. That was when he told me about the Midnight Stone. He said we could rule together, the spider and the fly – just imagine that!" She turned away, her back to them. "I declined his offer. While you were at each other's throats, I lay in wait. I planned how I could one day take the stone for myself. How I could take revenge on all ferals for the way they have treated us. Me, and my mother, and her mother before her."

"I don't even know who you *are*," said Selina's voice. Caw looked behind and saw she was in the doorway. She'd ditched her coat and was wearing a black T-shirt with frayed sleeves. Her eyes were red but full of anger.

Cynthia Davenport's sneer dropped a fraction. "You shouldn't be in here," she said.

"Well, forgive me, but I couldn't really concentrate on the DVD collection," said Selina. "Not with a rotting head in my eyeline."

"Sarcasm never suited you," said the Mother of Flies.

Selina looked around the room, with her lip curled. "I suppose this is where you come all the time, when you leave the house. When you're 'working late'. I'm supposed to be your *daughter*! I trusted you, and you used me."

"One day my gift will be yours," said the Mother of Flies. "Whether I like it or not."

Selina's face twisted. "You think I want to be like you?" she said. "You think I want any of this?" she added, waving a hand around the room. "You're doing all this because you're –" she paused, as if searching for the word – "you're *evil*."

The Mother of Flies narrowed her eyes, her face hardening. "If you had seen how low your ancestors fell, you'd be thanking me now. You never knew your grandmother. You never saw how all the self-righteous ferals shunned her, shuddered at the very sight of her. And when she was laid to rest in a pauper's grave, none came to her funeral. Not one. Even the centipede feral was buried with dignity! But for the fly talker... nothing but fear and hatred." She turned on Caw suddenly, gripping his face in her hand, grinding her fingers into his jaw. "Now, Jack, where is the Midnight Stone?"

Her nails cut into his cheeks.

"Get off him!" said Lydia. Mr Silk grabbed her before she could move.

The Mother of Flies stared into Caw's eyes as he writhed in her grip. He felt her gazing through them, her hunger burrowing in his mind.

"He knows," she said. "He *knows*."

With her free hand she seized his shoulder and pushed her thumb into the dislocated socket. Caw screamed and fell to his knees. "Tell me!" she shouted.

Caw felt dribble spooling from his mouth and he gasped in sheer agony. Any second now he would pass out. He couldn't have spoken even if he wanted to.

Cynthia Davenport released him and Caw collapsed on to his side, still reeling in pain. He saw the Mother of Flies give a small nod to Mr Silk and immediately the moth feral hoisted a screaming Lydia into the air, hooking her collar over one of the meat hooks. Mr and Mrs Strickham lunged to stop him, but Pinkerton already had a gun drawn and pointing at their heads.

Lydia squirmed like a fish out of water, her feet dangling in the air, her hands still trapped by the cuffs behind her back.

"Where is it, Caw?" said the Mother of Flies.

Caw didn't know what to do. Mrs Strickham glared at the barrel of Pinkerton's gun.

"Don't tell her!" shouted Lydia.

Cynthia Davenport whipped around, her face alive with anger. She threw out an arm and to Caw's horror it simply dissolved into a stream of flies, leaving her sleeve empty and drooping. The insects fell across Lydia's face and she screamed, whipping her head from side to side. The flies crawled, buzzing madly, into her open mouth. Lydia's screams turning to grunts and chokes, and her body jerked on the hook.

"Stop it, please!" cried Mr Strickham.

"All right! I'll tell you!" said Caw.

At once the flies streamed out of Lydia's mouth, swooping back to their mistress and disappearing into the front of her jacket. Her sleeve filled again and a pale hand appeared from the cuff. She sat down, folding one leg over the other.

"That's better, Caw," she said. "Now, you have one

169

opportunity to tell me the truth. If you lie, or attempt to deceive me in any way, the fox talker's daughter's last breath will be smothered in flies. Do you understand me?"

Caw shivered in the frigid air. "Yes," he said.

"So, where is the Midnight Stone?"

Caw swallowed, his mind desperately searching for a way out – some way to protect what his mother had entrusted to him. Lydia's face was mottled with fear. Mr Strickham was breathing heavily, his wife looking at the ground. No, there was no way out of here. No animals to call to their aid. The Mother of Flies had them right where she wanted them.

Caw fought against the despair that tried to tear him down. Why couldn't Bootlace have kept the stone for just a few days more? Why couldn't his mother have left him out of this? He wasn't a warrior feral, like the ones who'd fought in the Dark Summer. He was just a boy. He hadn't asked for any of this.

But he knew that wasn't an excuse and it echoed hollow in his heart. He'd let them down. His mother, his father, all the ferals who'd given their lives to protect what was good.

"Just tell her," said Mrs Strickham softly.

"Mum, no!" said Lydia.

"Well?" said the Mother of Flies, with a slow smile.

"It's buried in Blackstone Park," Caw said. "Under a bench near the bandstand."

Cynthia Davenport's eyes locked on to his for a few seconds.

"I'm telling the truth," he said.

The Mother of Flies nodded. "Yes, you are," she said, standing straighter. "Mr Silk, Pinkerton, come with me."

She strode towards the door, her cronies following at her heels. Selina remained motionless as though frozen with horror at what she had seen.

"You're despicable," spat Mrs Strickham at the fly feral. "And you won't win. Even if you find that stone and take away our powers, others will rise to fight you."

The Mother of Flies stopped and frowned.

"You think that's all I want? To take away your powers?" she said.

Caw felt a flicker of uncertainty. "That's what the stone does, isn't it?" he said.

Cynthia Davenport stared at him, as if she was genuinely confused. At last her eyes crinkled with a kind of cruel delight. "Oh, Caw. You poor child. It is so much more than that... You don't even know, do you?"

Caw didn't know what to say. He *thought* he knew, but what if he was wrong?

Cynthia Davenport's lips curled into a savage smile. "The Midnight Stone is –" she seemed to be hunting for the right word – "it is the *future*."

She left the room and the doors closed with a soft beep as the locking mechanism activated behind her.

Chapter 12

Selina slumped against the wall. "I'm so sorry," she muttered. She was trembling with cold in just her T-shirt, her lips purple. "I didn't know... about any of this."

Caw didn't care any more. What did it matter? They had lost and the Mother of Flies had won.

Mr Strickham rushed over and stood beneath Lydia.

"Put your feet on my shoulders," he said. Lydia did so, and with a bit of wriggling her collar tore off the hook. She fell to the ground in a heap.

"I'm all right," she said, struggling on to her knees with her hands still tied.

"Here, let me help with the cuffs," said Selina approaching.

"Get away from me!" shouted Lydia.

Selina paused.

"You have a key?" said Mrs Strickham.

Selina reached up into her hair and pulled out a spindly clip which she bent out of shape. "The next best thing."

Lydia looked like she wanted to punch Selina in the face.

"Let her help you," Caw said. "We need to work together now."

Mrs Strickham gave a brisk nod and Lydia turned her back so that Selina could get to the cuffs.

Selina took the cuffs softly and began to work with the end of the pin. It took a matter of seconds to get them off, but Lydia didn't say anything as they dropped to the floor.

Next Selina came to Caw. Her teeth were chattering and her hands were shaking as well. Their eyes met briefly, then he turned to let her remove the cuffs from behind his back. Even though she was gentle, he winced as pain shot through his shoulder like an electric current. Then the pressure on his wrists vanished with a soft click. "Thank you," he said.

Lydia's father had gone to the door to inspect the sensor pad. Meanwhile Mrs Strickham moved behind Caw. "We need to fix that shoulder of yours," she said. "Hold still." Before he could say anything, she'd wrapped one hand under his armpit and around his chest. With the other she grabbed his forearm. Caw cried out as she jerked his arm upwards. He staggered against the wall.

"There," said Mrs Strickham. "That should be better now."

As Caw took deep breaths and held his tender shoulder, Mrs Strickham took the pin from Selina's hand and went to work on her husband's cuffs. Caw let his head rest against the cool wall as the waves of throbbing pain subsided.

"So what now?" said Lydia. "We need to get out of here."

Mrs Strickham dropped the last set of cuffs on the floor and rubbed her hands together vigorously. "Agreed. It looks like we were wrong about the stone. Whatever it's capable of, it's worse than we thought."

Selina reached into her pocket and pulled out a card. "I think I can help."

"Is that what I think it is?" said Caw.

Selina nodded. "I took it off Mr Silk."

"Convenient," said Lydia.

Caw remembered how Selina had stolen his watch in their earlier encounter. "She's good at things like that."

Mr Strickham frowned at Selina. "Why should we trust you?"

She shrugged. "I don't care if you do or not. I'm getting out of here."

Lydia moved like a flash, snatching the card off her.

"Hey!" said Selina.

"You've done nothing but deceive us," said Lydia. "We should leave you in here."

For a moment, Caw thought Selina might fight back, so he stood between them.

"She didn't have to help us," he said to Lydia. "We can't let her freeze to death."

"The elevator," said Mr Strickham. "The guy in the white hat used the card there as well."

Lydia went to the door. "Let's go," she said.

Velma Strickham moved her gently aside. "Stay here until the coast is clear," she said to her daughter.

"But, Mum..."

"Do as your mother says," said Mr Strickham.

Caw drew the Crow's Beak and shot a glance at Selina. "Are you coming?"

Selina nodded, approaching the door cautiously.

"Don't worry," said Mr Strickham. "I don't bite."

"But my foxes do," said Mrs Strickham. "If you have second thoughts and try to betray us again, I won't think twice."

"Ready?" asked Lydia.

Caw nodded.

Lydia touched the card to the sensor and the door opened. The pig's head still sat on the table, but there were no flies any more. Caw guessed they must have flown off with their mistress. He crept out. The door to the bar was closed, but he could hear the raucous voices of the convicts on the other side.

If they could just keep quiet, they might make it out of here.

Selina pointed to the lounge area and Mrs Strickham nodded. They passed the fireplace. And then a high-backed chair shifted fractionally, and Pinkerton swivelled to face them. She was nibbling on a huge lump of cheese, but when she saw them she clambered to her feet, backing away. "Y-y-you!" she said.

Caw jumped at her, lunging with the Crow's Beak. She dropped her cheese, squealed and then she was on him, knocking him on to his back. Her teeth clamped over his wrist.

Caw opened his mouth in a silent roar as her hands clawed at his face...

Thump!

Pinkerton toppled sideways. Caw looked up to see Mr Strickham holding a table lamp and the rat feral out cold. As he clambered to his feet, Caw saw blood dripping from puncture wounds on his arm. He picked up the Crow's Beak. "Thank you," he whispered.

Mrs Strickham took hold of Pinkerton's feet and dragged her out of sight behind a sofa.

Selina led the way back across the apartment towards the stairs. Caw wondered if the Mother of Flies would have reached the park yet. On her own she could have, but to search the area properly, she'd have needed to take people with her. That meant they might still have a chance.

As they got to the stairs leading up to the walkway, Caw saw properly into the kitchen area for the first time. It was all sleek steel with dark stone tiling. He was about to follow Selina when he caught a movement at the far end and blinked in confusion. Mr Silk seemed to materialise out of the kitchen wall, moths twitching all over his suit. Caw realised they'd somehow been camouflaging him there. Mr Silk drew a gun from his jacket.

"Stop there!" snarled the moth feral.

"Run!" cried Caw, grabbing Lydia's hand.

A burst of gunfire exploded from the kitchen, smashing into the floor-to-ceiling windows on the other side of the apartment, sending spider-web cracks across the huge glass panes.

Selina leapt up the stairs, and Caw followed. But Lydia squirmed free from his grip. "Wait!" she said. Caw turned and saw Lydia's parents flailing as a swirling swarm of moths drove them back.

"Get off them!" screamed Lydia.

"Go!" said her father, trying to beat the moths back. "You won't get another chance!"

Lydia tried to run to them, but Caw pulled her back the other way.

"Listen to them," he said.

"No!" she shouted, struggling to break free. Selina grabbed her arm, trying to help, and Lydia wheeled around to hit her across the face. Selina caught her wrist in a strong grip and spoke through gritted teeth. "I know you don't like me, but I'm *trying* to save your life."

Mr Silk reached the bottom of the stairs and levelled the barrel of his gun. "Get back here!" he said.

Lydia struggled, but Selina was too strong.

"*Listen* to her," Caw said.

He saw his friend's arm loosen and Selina let go. Lydia took a last look back down the stairs then let him lead her on to the walkway, towards the lift.

She swiped the card against the sensor.

Nothing happened.

She swiped again.

Caw grabbed the card and tried, with the same result.

"There must be emergency stairs," said Selina. She pointed towards a door a few metres along the walkway. "What about in there?"

Caw could hear a trample of footsteps coming from somewhere else in the apartment. Shouts followed.

"Where are they?"

"Find 'em!"

"This way!"

Caw swung open the door and charged through. It was just another corridor lined with doors. He tried the first and it didn't open. He ran to the second, which did.

He skidded to a halt, as animal sounds assaulted his ears.

Howls and barks, hisses and chirrups and squawks came from cages lining the walls, stacked on top of one another and arranged into rows. What was this place? An owl watched them from a perch, and some sort of wild dog snarled above it. Caw crept forward along one of the aisles, keeping well clear. There was a black panther prowling back and forth, staring with emerald green eyes. A giant toad swelled its throat and watched them impassively. Two different kinds of monkey hung off a set of bars, gripping with furry fingers.

"Selina?" Caw asked. "What is this?"

Selina shook her head, her mouth slightly open in shock. "I have no idea."

They turned a corner and Caw paused at a tank containing a large wriggling centipede. Emily's creature. The rest of the row mostly seemed to be dogs, cats, snakes and rodents. A lizard, three feet long, tasted the air with a purple forked tongue.

The next cage was huge and empty, but the last one shook, and a deep growl came from inside. Caw brandished his sword as a bear pressed its snout against the mesh. It seemed almost unreal. How had Cynthia Davenport even got it into the building?

"Quick! They're coming!" said Lydia. The shouts and footsteps outside were getting closer.

There was nowhere to hide. Except...

Caw opened the empty cage door and they all piled in, pressed close. His heart throbbed and his grip was sweaty on the hilt of the Crow's Beak. He'd use it if he had to, but how many could he take on before they were overwhelmed?

The voices stopped as the convicts reached the door to the room. "They're not in here," said Lugmann. "Keep looking."

As soon as the convincts had gone, they all stepped out of the cage again.

Caw went back to the door and looked out. The convicts were moving on down the passage, and had almost rounded the corner at the far end when one of them turned back. His eyes settled on Caw.

"There they are!" he shouted, grinning.

Selina, Lydia and Caw raced out of the room and along the corridor to the walkway, then back down the steps and into the main area of the apartment again. When they arrived, breathless, Mr Silk had gone, along with Lydia's parents.

"Where are they?" cried Lydia, desperately.

Caw ignored her, looking at the glass of the window, splintered by Mr Silk's bullets.

He crossed to the coffee table and picked up a heavy bronze sculpture of a fly that squatted there, as big as his head. He hefted it to his shoulder. Then he closed his eyes and sent out his summons into the night. He wasn't sure how many he'd need. If the crows didn't hear him, they were all dead.

The air prickled with crow energy. They had heard, but they were distant.

Caw took a deep breath. Then he hurled the sculpture at the window. The entire pane of glass smashed outwards, and glittering fragments tumbled into the abyss. A fierce wind whipped through the apartment.

The convicts burst through the door above and spread out on the walkway. They clutched knives and guns, metal bars and baseball bats.

"Hold fire," said Lugmann. "They're trapped."

Caw thrust the Crow's Beak through his belt, and felt for Selina and Lydia's freezing hands. He stepped forward, leading them to the edge of the empty space where the window had been.

"You're going to have to trust me," he said quietly.

"Erm... What are you going to do?" said Selina.

"Ready?" said Caw.

"What are you going to do, jump?" laughed Lugmann. The other convicts joined in gleefully.

Lydia gripped Caw's hand harder. "I hope you know what you're—"

Caw leapt, dragging the two girls with him, his eyes searching the sky for a saviour.

His stomach flipped as they plummeted.

He couldn't see a single bird.

Chapter 13

Caw's body flailed and twisted and the world spun, flashing glass, then streaking city lights, then star-filled sky. Fear sucked at his insides. He was aware of Lydia and Selina falling too, but their hands were no longer in his.

We're dead. I've killed them...

Then impacts shook his body. Feathers and flashing beaks surrounded him. Pairs of eyes, steady and fearless. His own descent began to slow, but not fast enough. He was falling front-first, his legs gripped from behind, his jacket pulling against him as the crows tugged at his back. The ground rushed unstoppably towards him, and he tried to cover his face, but he couldn't move his arms as the crows had them too. The wind drove its thumbs into his eyes and tugged at his cheeks as he fell towards the ground, splayed, in the shape of a cross.

He felt the birds heaving and he heaved with them,

his desperation working through their wings. He closed his eyes.

His final thought swallowed everything else.

Pull!

The world tipped again and suddenly Caw's downward plunge curved into a shallower trajectory, fighting against gravity. As he opened his eyes he saw the concrete rush past beneath him as, at last, they began to climb.

He glanced across and saw Lydia and Selina dangling in the crows' grip too, a mixture of terror and triumph on their faces.

They steered in convoy, climbing steadily now. Caw looked back up to the apartment and saw the convicts standing at the open window, furiously clutching their weapons, and he felt his lips twitch into a smile.

Caw willed his crows to head northeast. They left the financial district behind and climbed higher into the clouds. Below, the city lights dipped in and out of sight.

"Where are we going?" called Selina over the wind. Her cheeks were flushed, her eyes shining.

"The park," said Caw. He just hoped they weren't too late.

Away from the city centre, the lights became more sparse. Here, in the outskirts, Blackstone slept.

The crows flew tirelessly, wings slicing through the

air in perfect synchronicity. Lydia hung mutely in their grip, but Caw could see from her haunted expression that her mind was restless, thinking of her parents. He wanted to comfort her and tell her that they'd be all right, but he knew his words would sound unconvincing. The problem was he didn't believe it himself.

When they neared the park, Caw saw that the gates were open. A bad sign. He commanded his crows to keep a distance from the bandstand as the flock carried them over the park's perimeter, and Caw saw the trees and small lakes wheel below. From a couple of hundred feet away, he could see there were bright lights around the bandstand already, and several police cars, and his heart sank.

"She beat us to it," Lydia said.

"We need to get closer," Caw replied. "Hold on."

The crows obeyed his thoughts, dipping sharply. Selina gasped as the flock swept over the ground, slaloming between the trees, so low Caw's feet almost brushed the grass. He trusted the birds, but Lydia pulled up her legs, tucking her knees to her chest.

Tilting their wings, the birds banked and rose towards the branches of one of the tallest trees in the park – one that Caw knew well. He saw his old abandoned nest, its collection of timbers coming apart, the tarpaulin torn and dangling over the side. The birds hovered for a moment a couple of feet above, then dropped the girls inside. Lydia staggered and caught herself against the edge of the treehouse. Selina landed more neatly, bending her knees.

Caw's crows set him down gently, then flocked away into the branches. He focused on one – a small male with a slender beak – and called out to him.

Me, boss? it said.

"I need you to find out what's happening at the bandstand," said Caw. "Stay hidden if you can."

Sure thing, said the crow, puffing out its chest, then springing upwards. Caw watched its black shape flap away until it folded seamlessly into the night.

"What is this place?" Selina said, gazing around.

"This is where I grew up," said Caw. He felt a flash of pride.

"We can't just sit around," said Lydia. "My parents are in trouble!"

"She won't really kill them," said Selina, reaching to touch Lydia's arm.

Lydia slapped her hand away. "What do you know?" she said. "Wake up, will you?"

"What's that supposed to mean?" asked Selina.

"It *means*," said Lydia, "that your mum's a psycho. And how do we really know you're any better?"

"Now isn't the time for this," said Caw.

"Why not?" said Lydia. She jabbed a finger towards Selina. "We should have left you there. I swear, if she hurts my mum and dad, I'll..."

"You'll what?" said Selina, drawing herself up.

Lydia fell silent, glaring. Her cheekbones were tinged with red.

The crow fluttered back to the nest's edge. *The ground by the bench is all dug up*, it said. *The police are leaving now.*

Caw felt like curling into a ball and wailing with frustration. But what good would it do? If the police were going, it could only mean that the Mother of Flies had found the Midnight Stone.

"She's got it, hasn't she?" said Selina.

Caw nodded.

Why the long faces? said another crow voice. Glum landed in the nest.

"Glum!" said Caw. "Where've you been?"

Screech flew in too, and settled beside Lydia. *Here and there*, he said. *Who's this?* he demanded, jabbing his beak towards the crow who'd scouted the bandstand.

Just helping out the boss, said the crow.

"Where's Shimmer?" asked Caw.

She's lagging behind a bit, said Glum. *Got her talons full.*

Caw frowned. "What do you mean?"

Screech started hopping excitedly and Glum looked particularly smug.

"What are they saying?" asked Lydia.

"Come on," Caw said. "Spit it out."

When we saw you on the tracks, and the fly feral wanted to know where the Midnight Stone was... began Glum.

...well, we had an idea, added Screech.

Maybe we'd move the stone, said Glum.

"You didn't?" said Caw, fighting the urge to smile.

Shimmer swooped overhead, flapping her wings hard. Something glinted in her talons. *Why'd I have to do all the heavy lifting?* she called down. *Here, catch!*

She dropped the Midnight Stone and it landed in the nest, clattering to rest on the wooden boards.

Shimmer flopped down next to it, wings spread. *Phew. I'm done!*

Caw took the handkerchief from his pocket and picked up the stone. Just holding it filled him with relief. He hadn't failed. But it was more than that. It made him feel strangely... whole.

"I could hug you all!" he said.

It was Shimmer's idea, said Screech, pointing his wing.

Suck-up, muttered Glum.

"So what now?" said Lydia. "Do we offer her a trade?"

Caw's fist closed over the stone. "We can't," he said.

"Why not?" said Lydia. "That's all she wants – that stupid stone."

Caw looked at his friend. "Exactly," he said. "Remember what your mother said. It's *all* she wants. Our lives mean nothing to her."

"Caw's right," said Selina.

Lydia glared at her. "No one asked what you thought."

"Lydia, we can't risk it," said Caw. He saw her face twitch slightly and he knew she was wavering. "Think about it. What's really changed?" he asked. "She has what we want. We have what she wants."

"Stalemate," said Selina.

Lydia tore her eyes from Selina back to Caw. "Maybe you're right. But we can't just sit up a tree doing nothing."

Caw lifted the stone in front of his face. He looked again for some clue in its surface, but there was nothing.

"Maybe it's time to find out what this thing is," he said. "What it *really* is. No more secrets."

"My mum didn't know anything about it," said Lydia.

"My mum seems to be the only person who *does*," said Selina.

"There's someone else," said Caw. "Felix Quaker."

Lydia looked unconvinced. "You really think he might be able to help?"

Hah! said Screech. *He couldn't get away fast enough last time he saw it.*

"We've got to try," said Caw. "He won't be at his house though. He was terrified. The police were looking for him."

"Typical," said Lydia. "For a man who's supposed to have nine lives, he doesn't like to put himself in harm's way, does he?"

What about all his books? said Glum. *Surely there'll be something in one of them.*

"Good thinking," said Caw. "Let's go."

He stepped to the edge of the nest, motioning for Selina and Lydia to join him. His body ached, but a fire still burnt somewhere inside him. He reached out his arms and summoned his crows once more.

Chapter 14

The crows flew low and fast. Quaker's place was a long shot, but Caw remembered how it had been stuffed with artefacts and books, like a museum. Glum was right – there *had* to be a clue there somewhere.

As they approached Gort House, Caw's hopes evaporated. The gates were still hanging open and now police tape was stretched across.

The crows set them down in the driveway. Caw ducked beneath the tape slowly, and crept towards the house, the girls following behind him. All the lights were off.

Looks deserted, said Screech, skittering to a halt on the gravel.

The crow was right. If the police had been here again, it looked like they were long gone. "Let's go in carefully," he said.

The crows touched down silently across the ornamental gardens.

"Wait out here and keep your eyes peeled for flies," he said.

No way – I'm coming in, said Shimmer, hopping ahead.

Not without me you're not, said Screech, limping to keep up.

Well, I'll *do as I'm told*, said Glum, settling on top of a bush.

There was more tape over the front door, which was hanging on one hinge from where the police had smashed it down. Caw remembered the cops' brutality in arresting Quaker. Back then he'd thought they were just being heavy-handed, but now he realised it was personal – an order from the top.

"Is this guy some sort of criminal?" said Selina.

"More like an academic," said Caw. "Quaker collects feral artefacts. Your mother must have thought that Quaker could help her find the stone. Or me, at least."

He tore the tape aside. "Felix?" he called.

His voice echoed in the cold hallway and no one replied. Hardly surprising.

Inside, the wooden floorboards creaked slightly underfoot. A mahogany staircase rose then turned to the first floor. Dirty footprints muddied the once pristine carpet. To the left, Caw saw Quaker's study – desk drawers hanging out and papers littering the floor. Ash and blackened wood was smeared across the rug in front of the hearth and a lamp lay smashed on the floor.

The police had even torn the pictures from the walls.

Caw led the others down a narrow set of stairs towards the kitchen. As he descended, a curious feeling of loss swept over him. It was here that Quaker had told Caw about his parents and his true name – Jack Carmichael. It was the first time he had really ever felt a sense of belonging and connection to the city that existed around him.

He owed the old man for that, at least.

The kitchen was empty too, but a plate of chopped apples and what might have been cheese and bread lay on the table, half-eaten and growing a skin of furry mould across its surface. The teapot had been knocked over.

"Looks like he never came back," said Lydia.

Caw cast a quick glance around. "He was obviously really scared. Let's check the rest of the place."

"The study seemed promising," said Lydia.

"OK," said Caw. "Let's start in there."

"I'll go upstairs," said Selina.

Lydia frowned.

"Seriously," said Selina. "You honestly think I'm going to run?"

"Shout if you find anything," said Caw, as Selina set off up the stairs.

Caw and Lydia went to the study. The police had obviously done a thorough job going through the place, but it was possible they'd missed something. They began to sift through the mess. A lot of the documents were handwritten notes, completely indecipherable, even for Lydia.

"This is hopeless," she said, tossing a piece of paper aside.

"Just keep looking," said Caw, checking the drawers.

But as the minutes passed, his despair grew. What was the chance, really, that they'd find anything?

"I'm going upstairs," he said.

Lydia puffed out her cheeks. "OK," she said, squinting at a page. "I'm not sure this is even in English!"

Caw trooped up the wide stairwell with Shimmer flapping ahead. More pictures had been taken down, their canvasses slit and their frames broken. Where Caw remembered display cases filled with curious objects, now there was only broken glass crunching underfoot. The whole collection was gone – years of work. If Quaker saw what they'd done, he would be inconsolable.

He came across Selina in what must have been Felix's bedroom, which was just as ransacked as everywhere else. She was sitting on a bedframe rifling through a pile of papers on the dressing table. A chest of drawers had been dismantled and clothes were strewn across the floor. A wardrobe lay on its side and the mattress had been slashed apart. From the ceiling hung a bare light fitting and the carpet had been pulled up in places, revealing damp floorboards.

"Find anything?" he asked.

She shook her head, and Caw noticed suddenly that she was trying to stop herself crying.

"Selina?" he said.

What's she got to be so sad about? said Shimmer.

Caw pointed downstairs. "Give me some privacy, will you?" he muttered.

As Shimmer flew away, he went into the room, and sat beside her on the edge of the bed. He saw that the papers were just old bills.

"I suppose I've always known," she said quietly. "Not that she was a feral. But that she was... not nice."

"Your mother?"

"Ha!" Selina barked a laugh. "*Mother!* She loves those flies more than me."

Caw put a hand on her shoulder. He wanted to comfort her, but he hardly knew how.

"She fooled a lot of people," he said.

Selina sniffed. "We were never close," she said. "I went to boarding school at five, and even in the holidays she was mostly working. I used to stay with aunts and uncles. Or play by myself. When she said she had an important job for me, I said I'd do it straight away. I guess I just wanted her to notice me."

Caw stood there, awkwardly, with his hand still resting on her shoulder.

"I know how you feel," he said. "I never really knew

my parents. I always thought they were one thing, when they were something else completely."

"Your parents were good people," said Selina. "My mother is evil."

"But you're not," said Caw. He reached to touch her hand, but stopped himself.

Selina looked up at him. "You mean that?" she said. "After everything?"

Caw imagined what Velma Strickham would say. *She's the Mother of Flies' daughter – she cannot be your friend.*

But he wasn't the fox feral.

"I do," he said.

Lydia coughed from the doorway, and Caw and Selina broke apart. "Sorry to interrupt your little... whatever this is," she said.

Caw shrugged. "It's fine. Any good news?"

Lydia shook her head and gestured back over her shoulder. "The library's there though. Got to be worth a look."

They followed her across the landing. Inside, the bookshelves had been pulled down and they lay across mountains of leather-bound volumes. "We might be here a while," said Lydia.

Caw was just about to reach for a book when a soft *miaow* made them all jump. A single grey cat stood behind them in the doorway.

"Hello, kitty," said Selina.

The cat stared at them a moment, blue eyes shining with intelligence. Then it padded silently towards them. Shimmer jumped off the floor, flapping.

The cat ignored the crows and entwined itself with Selina's legs. She stroked the top of its head. "Is she a stray, do you think?" asked Selina.

"No," said Caw, frowning as he recognised the cat. It was the one that had been hurled off the car bonnet by the policeman. "*He* belongs to Felix Quaker. His name is Freddie."

Selina was crouching, fiddling with his collar. "That isn't what it says here." She squinted and the cat purred. "The little tag says its name is 'Wythe'."

"Are you sure?" said Lydia.

Selina gave her a sharp look. "Yes, I *can* read."

The cat hopped up on to one of the fallen bookcases and approached Caw. Its striking blue eyes watched him closely.

"What do you think, Screech?" Caw said. "He's the one from outside, isn't he?"

Looks like it to me, said Screech, keeping his distance.

"I wonder why he's stayed here?" said Lydia. "I would have thought Quaker would take all his cats with him."

"Freddie?" said Caw. The cat brushed against him, arching its spine. "Perhaps this is Quaker's way of offering help," he said.

Fat lot of good one mog's going to be, said Shimmer.

"No," said Caw. "I mean, a message of some sort. If he was too frightened to help us face to face."

Optimistic, said Glum.

Caw looked at the metal tag. Sure enough, someone had scratched away some writing on one side of the tag. On the other, carved roughly, were the letters of the word 'Wythe'.

"It looks like it was done in a hurry," said Caw. He stared at the word, certain he'd read it before – but where?

Never heard of a Wythe, said Screech.

The cat hissed and placed its paw on Caw's sleeve.

Maybe he just wants food, said Screech. *You know what cats are like – loyal to anyone who'll feed them. Not like crows...*

Caw tried to focus on the name in his mind's eye. He searched his memory for its presence and imagined Quaker there too, urging him on: "Come on, lad. Use your brain! It's right in front of you..."

Caw felt a smile tickling his lips. Now he remembered where he knew the word "Wythe" from. He had *seen* it – the letters in a looping script. And it made perfect sense.

What are you grinning like a mad fool for? asked Screech.

Clever, clever Quaker!

"I think I know where we can find out about the stone," he said.

Chapter 15

Great banks of grey cloud lay sprawled across the night sky, blotting out the stars. The wind whipped around their bodies as the birds carried them to the edge of the city.

Will there be worms? said Screech.

"I hope so," said Caw. "But you'll have to control yourself. If we find Bootlace, he probably won't take kindly to you eating his creatures."

He won't notice if one or two go missing, said Shimmer.

If he even is where you think he is, said Glum. *Seems like a long shot to me.*

"No, it's not," said Caw.

The words of the worm feral were still fresh in his mind. *Closer to her than ever now, of course.*

It had seemed odd at the time, but Caw had been in such a state of shock that he'd not paid much attention. It made sense though.

His mother was dead. Her body was buried in the same churchyard outside the city as Emily the centipede feral. And that was where Caw had seen the name Wythe. What could be closer to his mother than the resting place beside her own?

They descended to the graveyard, on the other side of the church from Emily's tomb. Caw's murder of crows let his feet touch the ground softly and released their hold. The girls landed at his side.

"I could get used to this," said Lydia, smiling broadly.

The crows all circled the looming church, then fell in a synchronised descent, alighting across the headstones. The trees in the graveyard shivered in a gust of wind.

"Are you sure about this?" said Selina. "I mean, seriously, what sort of freak lives in a graveyard?"

"I don't think you need to be speaking about freaks," said Lydia. "Your mum's so-called 'study' is a slaughter-house."

Caw saw a flash of pain across Selina's face.

"I guess I asked for that," she said quietly.

Caw frowned at Lydia, who just shrugged back. He frowned harder and she sighed.

"I'm sorry," she said. "That was mean of me."

"It's OK," said Selina. "Let's find this grave, shall we?"

Caw marched between the headstones, past the spot where his parents were buried. Two over, near to the low wall that ran around the edge of the church grounds, was another headstone lying on its back, covered in a skein of lichen and blotted with age. The name "Henry Wythe" was engraved across the top.

"This is it!" said Caw. "I knew I was right."

The rest of the writing was hard to read, so Caw carefully scraped away a patch of moss beneath the name. *1642–1734.*

"Wow! It's old," said Selina. "I didn't even know Blackstone was here that long ago."

There was more writing, and though Caw could make out the letters, he couldn't make much sense of the words. "What does it say?" he asked.

"What, can't you read?" said Selina.

Caw blushed. "I'm learning."

"So what if he can't?" snapped Lydia. "His parents never taught him, all right?"

"Oh... OK," said Selina. "Sorry." She squinted as she read. "It says, 'Gilded tombs do worms enfold.'"

"Worms!" said Caw. "It must be the place! But – what does that mean?"

"I guess," said Lydia, "it means even if you have a fancy grave, you're no better than everyone else. Everyone ends up as worm food once they've been buried."

"Maybe not the worm feral himself though," said Caw.

It's a three hundred year old grave, not a house, said Screech. *Am I missing something?*

Almost always, sniggered Glum.

Now Caw looked closer, he could see there were sculpted worms on the face of the stone and more trailing over the edges. He dropped on to his knees and let his hands search around the rim.

There had to be something. Some clue.

"Are you sure this is right?" said Selina, looking around anxiously. "I mean, I like graveyards as much as the next girl, but—"

"Just let him get on with it," said Lydia.

Click-thunk.

One of the stone worms moved under Caw's fingertips, pressing into the headstone, and the whole thing shifted a fraction. Caw drew back his hands.

"You were saying, Screech?" he said.

"It's a door!" said Selina. Caw nodded, then stood with his fingers in the tiny gap between the headstone and the earth. He heaved, and the stone lifted up on some sort of hinge. Bits of soil and grass tumbled into a black hole beneath.

Not underground again... muttered Glum, flapping to the edge.

Caw let the headstone rest upright. On the underside was a handle, so that someone within could push it open. Steep stone steps led downwards into the ground.

"You two should stay out here," he said to Lydia and Selina.

"No way!" they said at the same time, then scowled at each another.

"Fine," said Caw. "But be careful, and stay behind me."

Shimmer peered over the edge, and shuddered.

"You don't have to come either," said Caw.

She tossed her beak. *Wouldn't miss it for the world,* she said breezily.

Don't worry, said Screech, brushing up alongside her. *I'll watch out for you.*

What a gallant! said Glum from above.

Caw stepped into the open grave. He had to stoop to get under the lip. The walls were bare earth, packed hard.

"I hope you're here, Bootlace," he murmured to himself.

He counted nineteen steps until he reached a passage. Selina came next, with Lydia and the crows at the rear. The air was musty and cold, and the light filtering from the hatch above barely penetrated the gloom. Lydia rummaged in her pocket and took out a mobile phone.

"I doubt you'll have a signal," said Selina.

Lydia gave her a contemptuous stare and pressed a button. Torchlight shone from the back of the phone and she moved it to face down the tunnel, catching the glinting eyes of the crows.

Caw gasped. The tunnel was about five feet in height, following a gentle downward slope. The walls and ceiling were reinforced with pieces of timber. He wondered if this place had been here as long as the gravestone above.

"Follow me," he said, setting off deeper into the earth.

The torchlight only reached about twenty feet and Caw strained his eyes at what might be beyond. He thought about drawing the Crow's Beak, but if they did meet Bootlace, it would be best to be unarmed. From time to time, a small pink head wriggled out of the walls, before retreating again. The crows managed to restrain themselves, thankfully.

Bootlace has spies everywhere, Caw thought.

Soon the light picked out a door ahead and Caw stopped beside it. The surface was gnarled wood, the planks fastened together with ironwork. Caw was no expert, but it looked hundreds of years old.

He pushed it open and sucked in a breath at the sight before him.

A huge cavern stretched out ahead – roofed with uneven stone, and filled in the centre with a lake so still it might have been polished glass. Hundreds of alcoves had been carved into the walls, and in each one a candle glowed. The flames reflected like orange starlight in the surface of the water.

Lydia bumped into Caw and pocketed her phone.

"This place is amazing!" she said. Selina was open-mouthed, craning her neck.

Let me see! Let me see! squawked Screech, hopping between their feet.

Caw walked forward slowly. All around the outside of the lake were tomb stones, some grand sarcophagi and others humble headstones. It was another graveyard, mirroring the one at ground level. But without the wind and rain of Blackstone weathering their surfaces, these tombs remained pristine – marble blazing in the candlelight. And instead of statues of cherubs, or angels, or engravings of flowers, they were decorated with animals. A perching falcon, so lifelike it looked ready to spread its wings; a lion standing proudly over a coffin; a wild boar with jutting tusks.

Something moved near Caw's foot. He glanced down and saw a worm the size of a small snake wrapping itself around his ankle, its pink flesh caked with crumbs of dirt. He cried out and stumbled, only for another to break the ground. Then another. They twitched and writhed blindly.

Something else darted from his left and Selina screamed. Caw turned to see a dark shape crouching against the wall.

"What do you want?" hissed the worm feral. He was still dressed in black, like he had been the night Caw had first met him.

Caw sensed the crows spreading their wings and stilled them with a thought. *Not yet.*

"I needed to see you..." he said.

The worm feral blinked his eyes, no longer concealed

by glasses as they had been outside the old house. Caw realised that they were pale orbs, with no irises or pupils.

He must be totally blind.

"It's me, Elizabeth Carmichael's son," said Caw.

The feral unfurled his body slowly, sniffing the air. "I know who *you* are," he said, "but who are they?" He jerked his head towards Lydia and Selina. "Enemies, come to prise me out of my hole, are they?"

"They're my friends," said Caw.

"But *she's* not *my* friend," said Lydia.

"They're no threat," Caw added. He made a face at Lydia to say *now is* not *the time!*

The worm feral edged a little closer, keeping his hands against the wall. His fingernails, Caw noticed, were sharp, and caked with dirt. The worms at Caw's feet burrowed into the ground and disappeared. "I am not afraid," he said. "What have I to fear? It is you who should tremble, mortal children."

"Mr Wythe..." said Caw, "or should I call you, Bootlace?"

"Call me what you will, crow talker," said the worm feral. "I've been known by more names than I can remember."

"These are feral graves, aren't they?" asked Caw.

Bootlace nodded. "Since the founding of the city, I have been the custodian of this place. What better person to watch over the dead than one who can never count death's blessings?"

"So wait – you can't *die*?" said Selina.

"No," said Bootlace. "And believe me, I have tried. No water can drown me, no fall can break my body. No poisons or weapons can bring the darkness I crave."

We're getting nowhere, said Shimmer. *Wythe's a nutjob.*

"I need to know about the Midnight Stone," said Caw.

"And how should I know anything about that, crow talker?"

The blunt tone took Caw by surprise.

"Because you gave it to me," he said.

"I was merely looking after it," said Bootlace. "Your mother gave you the stone."

"So you have no idea what it does?" said Selina.

"Perhaps I did, once," said Bootlace. "But I have chosen not to remember. One mind can only carry so much pain. So many deaths, each one as inevitable as the sunset. Only the worms remember all."

"Do worms have memories then?" asked Lydia.

Bootlace turned on her and Lydia stumbled back into Selina, who shoved her off. The worm feral jabbed a fingernail towards them both. "The worms *are* memories, foolish child," he said.

Anyone else thinking he's not making a lot of sense? asked Shimmer.

I'm with you, said Screech.

"Well, could I, uh... can I talk to them?" said Caw. "The worms, that is."

I can't believe you just said that, muttered Glum.

Bootlace snarled. "Why should they talk to you?" he said. "Crows are not favourites with worms, you know."

This is a waste of time, Caw, said Screech. *Worms are good for one thing – dinner.*

But Caw wasn't ready to be turned back. "I came here because you're my only chance," he said. "My mother must have trusted you for a reason. The Mother of Flies wants the Midnight Stone, and I need to know why."

Bootlace chuckled. "The fly talker? No need to worry about her, I'm sure. The fly line are carrion-feeders, the lowest of the low."

"It's not like that," said Lydia. "She's trying to take over the city."

"How the times change!" said Bootlace. "Well, I am safe down here, I suppose."

Caw tried not to let his impatience show. "Please," he said. "Can't you tell us anything?"

"I cannot remember," said Bootlace. "Your concerns might seem great to you, but for me they are trifles."

"Oh, you're hopeless," said Lydia fiercely. "Just a selfish old man."

"When you have lived as long as I have," said Bootlace, "your *self* is all you have."

Caw's frustration was reaching a boiling point. There

had to be some way to convince him. And then, suddenly, he realised there was. He reached over his shoulder and drew the Crow's Beak. Selina gasped. "Caw, you can't!"

"A sword?" said the worm feral with a snarl. "Blades do not frighten me, boy. I have seen many in my time."

"This isn't a sword for hurting people," said Caw. "It can rip a doorway through to oblivion. To the Land of the Dead."

As he raised the sword, the ground stirred, and thousands of worms broke through. There were so many, the air *rustled* with the sound of their bodies. Bootlace stood up, eyes fixed on the sword as if mesmerised.

"Would you really do this for me?" he said. "End my torment? Help me leave this world for the next?"

Caw nodded. "I'll help you to die. But first, help me."

The worms' bodies writhed, standing upright like feelers in the air.

Bootlace gestured to the rock on which he had been sitting. "Very well, crow talker. Take a seat and journey into a world of memory."

Caw edged forward and sat down on the cold rock, leaning the Crow's Beak against it. He glanced at Lydia and Selina, who both looked worried. Bootlace crouched, gently scooping several thin worms from the ground. He cupped them near to his mouth and whispered something.

"They will tell you," he said. Bootlace took one of the worms between his thumb and forefinger and dangled it at the side of Caw's head. Caw shifted away. "What are you doing?"

Bootlace grinned, revealing his dagger-like teeth. "Worms speak quietly, child. To hear them you must be prepared to listen. Now hold still. This may feel a little strange."

Even the crows were silent for once. Caw felt the worm tickle the cartilage of his ear, then squirm into his earhole. His skin crawled, but he managed to stay still. The look on Lydia's face was pure disgust.

Caw tried to ignore the sensation that the worm was burrowing into his brain, as Bootlace fed another into his ear. He swallowed. A sound like waves washing over shingle filled his head. He could feel every squirm as the worms forced their pulsing flesh into his ear canal.

"Are you all right?" said Lydia, her voice distant. "You've gone very pale."

The cavern blurred, and the shapes of Lydia and Caw and Bootlace doubled, then tripled. "What's happening to me?" Caw muttered.

Bootlace's laughter cackled and echoed. "Let them show you, crow talker. Don't fight it."

The images spun together so their shapes and colours melded. Caw felt himself falling backwards, and hands caught him, soft as cushions.

Caw closed his eyes and gave himself to the worms.

Chapter 16

When Caw opened his eyes again, Lydia and Selina and the crows were gone. He sat alone in the cave, surrounded by feral tombs. A worm played over the back of his hand.

No, not his hand. The skin was pale, the knuckles like knots of protruding bone, the nails filthy with dirt. Bootlace's hand. Caw tried to move it, but couldn't. He was trapped in a body not his own.

In a memory, he realised.

He could hear footsteps, coming from the passage. His body shrank away, carrying him into the shadows where he crouched, watching the door. He felt afraid.

The door opened, and a face appeared. Caw's heart jolted, almost painfully.

Mum?

She looked terrified, her hair a tangled mess, and a bruise across her cheek.

Caw longed to run to her, but his feet – Bootlace's feet – stayed rooted to the floor.

"Mr Wythe?" said his mother. "Are you here?"

"What do you want?"

The words came from within and without. He felt his lips move, but the voice was not his.

His mother squinted into the gloom. On her shoulder was a huge black crow missing a patch of feathers from its neck. It squawked, but Caw didn't understand what it was saying. "Mr Wythe – I need your help," said his mother. "May I come in?"

"If you must, crow talker."

Elizabeth Carmichael was wearing a bulky coat with a fur-lined hood, leather boots and long, delicate-looking gloves. She entered cautiously.

"Mr Wythe, I don't have long," said Caw's mother. She reached into her pocket and drew out a small drawstring bag. Caw could tell what was inside from the shape of it. The Midnight Stone. "You know what this is and the power it has."

Caw felt Bootlace flinch and draw back. He could tell that the worm feral *did* know – just – though the memory was a dim and dream-like one. "Why have you brought it here?"

"I need you to look after it for me," said Caw's mother, holding out the bag. Her eyes were desperate.

Bootlace made no move to take it. "The Midnight

Stone belongs with the crow line," he said.

"I know that," said Caw's mother, "but the spider feral has learnt of its existence."

"How?" said Bootlace. "The stone is a secret kept between crows and worms alone."

"That's not important," said Caw's mother, casting a glance back towards the door. "The Spinning Man will stop at nothing to have it. Please, you must."

Bootlace edged forward. He pulled his sleeve down over his hand. "Very well," he said, taking the bag. "And if you do not return? I have heard of the war that rages in Blackstone – many have perished already."

"I have a son – Jack," said Caw's mother. "Take it to him when the city is safe."

She folded Bootlace's sleeve-covered fingers over the bag and squeezed them tight. "You must tell him what it can do. He must tell no one about it. Trust no one. It is his to bear alone."

"I will tell him, crow talker," said Bootlace.

"Thank you." Caw's mother turned to go and Caw longed to go after her, to call out her name.

At the door, she stopped and turned, and for the briefest moment Caw wondered if she sensed his presence within the worm feral. But how could she? This was only a memory.

"Farewell, Mr Wythe," she said.

"Farewell, Elizabeth Carmichael," he said. "And fear not death. Remember, we are but food for worms."

"Easy for you to say," she replied. A wave of sadness passed over her face. "Remember, his name is Jack."

"We will remember," said Bootlace.

As the door closed behind her, the vision vanished. Caw felt his mind untether, and drift on seas of time...

He was looking into a fire, blazing in a hearth. The heat warmed his face and a grand tall clock was ticking slowly. The time read close to twelve o'clock.

His body turned and he saw a window of small, leaded panes black with night. He was standing in a study with wood panelling on the walls and oil paintings in gilt frames. A crowd of people – men and women of all ages – filled the room and talked to one another in hushed tones.

The gathering seemed to include those from all walks of life. He saw a small man in a rough-hewn brown jacket and dirt-streaked shirt, and a woman in a grand ballooning dress with a hat trailing lace. Others wore doublets or leather jerkins, work boots or shoes with polished buckles. One old man carried a cane topped with gold. Caw didn't know much about historical dress, but he guessed he was looking at a scene from several centuries ago. The only light came from candles on the walls and the fire in the grate.

A man cleared his throat and the crowd settled down, all turning towards him.

"Thank you for coming here tonight," he said.

Through the other people, Caw saw the speaker. He was a broad-shouldered man dressed entirely in black, with a tight-fitting velvet doublet, trousers and boots. His long wavy hair was black as well, swept away from his face, which was matted with a thick beard. A vertical scar ran over his left eye from the centre of his forehead to his cheek. At his hip hung a scabbard, and in it was a sword Caw knew well – the Crow's Beak.

Was this a crow feral? It had to be. He held the gaze of all the ferals in the room, seeming more real, somehow more *present*, than all of them. It wasn't just his striking black clothes that set him apart, or his fierce demeanour – he seemed to emanate a hidden power.

"The Winter Solstice is upon us," said the man. "It is a sacred time for our kind, but never have we been in greater danger."

The others in the room muttered to themselves and nodded.

The woman in the elaborate hat spoke up. "They're killing us, Corvus. Burning us at the stake as witches. Driving us from our homes."

Black Corvus! Quaker had told Caw about him; that he was the greatest of the crow line. Caw gazed at the grim face of his ancestor, hard as iron, looking for any similarity to his own.

The murmurings increased in volume, until Black Corvus raised his hands for silence. The room obeyed at once.

"People fear what they do not understand," he said. "And this is why I have summoned you here." He turned to a table and opened a plain wooden box. Inside, on a bed of white satin, was a black stone. It looked identical to the one Caw had in his possession.

Caw sensed Bootlace craning his neck to get closer. "Is that what I think it is?" he said.

Black Corvus's nostrils flared and he nodded. "It is Obdurian stone," he said.

Everyone in the room instantly backed away, and one or two crossed themselves.

"Black diamond!" said one of the gathering angrily. "What is the meaning of this?"

"It has taken me months to find it, deep beneath the ground," said Black Corvus. "It shall be our salvation."

"How can you say such a thing?" said the old man with the gold-tipped cane. "Obdurian saps the power of any feral who touches it, Corvus. It draws out our abilities, eroding the connection to our animals."

"Exactly," said Black Corvus. "And that is why I have brought it here. Take heed, friends, we have lost too many lines already. I ask each of you tonight – sacrifice some of your great powers, confer your gifts upon the stone, so that should you die without an heir, the line will not end."

"We will be weaker," said the scruffy man.

"But stronger as well," said the crow feral. "We will insure against our own demise."

The assortment of ferals were silent.

"I will be the first," said Black Corvus. Caw saw the eyes of the room follow the crow feral as he reached out. His hand was trembling, and as he touched the stone with his fingertips he closed his eyes. Caw saw pale threads of light penetrating the stone, which glowed momentarily before fading to black again. Black Corvus stepped away. "It is done," he said. "I beg you all, do the same. This is the only way to guarantee our survival."

One by one, the other ferals approached, and repeated the ceremony. Caw came last of all, in Bootlace's body, but Black Corvus shut the box before he could touch it.

"Your powers are not required, Henry," he said. "Your line will never be destroyed, as you cannot die."

"Thank you for reminding me," said Bootlace and, even in the distant memory, Caw felt an echo of loneliness and pain.

The clock struck the hour and twelve chimes rang out.

"We will call it the Midnight Stone," said Black Corvus

to the room. "Should any of you die without an heir, your abilities will live on in the stone. All that will be needed for a new feral to be born is for a new heir and their creature to come together in the presence of the stone."

In the back of Caw's mind, a fear took hold and festered. So that was the stone's true power... Not merely to take away a feral's abilities, but to bestow them too. The power to create new ferals. That was what the Mother of Flies had fought, kidnapped and killed for.

"And who will look after it?" said the man with the embossed cane. "If it should fall into the wrong hands..."

"With your blessing," said Black Corvus, looking around the room, "that duty will fall to me. I will never touch it, never giving up any more of my power to it, and never allowing any power to be taken from it."

A few people muttered, but the only one to speak up was a woman with a thin, angular face and fair hair that fell completely straight from a centre parting. "And after you, Corvus?"

"The Midnight Stone will be passed through the crow line," said the crow feral. "Not one of you in this room must ever mention it again." He brought out a scroll. "This is a pledge to keep what has happened here a secret in your hearts. With your deaths, the secret dies too, kept only by my descendants. And we will protect it to our dying breath. Until the time comes for the stone to be used."

"Noble words, Corvus," said the woman. "But would it not be better with him?" She pointed to Caw. "After all, the worm feral will always know the secret."

Caw sensed Bootlace's panic. "I am no warrior, miss," he said. "There is none better than Corvus to guard the stone."

Caw saw Black Corvus give him a nod of appreciation.

One by one, everyone in the room stepped forward to sign the parchment. Caw came last, in Bootlace's body. As he dipped the quill into the ink, the vision faded from his eyes.

Caw was breathing hard as slowly the candlelit tomb of the ferals swam back into focus. He fumbled with his ear and tugged out the wriggling tail of the worm, dropping it to the ground at his feet where the other one already lay.

He struggled to stand, but his legs were wobbly. The fear from the vision reignited inside his heart. The convicts in the apartment, the animals in the cages...

"I know... I know what she wants," said Caw. "I know what the Mother of Flies is planning."

"Be careful," said Bootlace. "Your mind is still in the past."

"What did you see?" asked Lydia.

"The Midnight Stone doesn't just take powers from ferals," he said. "That's only part of what it does. It can also *create* feral lines. Any feral line that's died out over the years – it can bring their powers back. That's why the Mother of Flies has all those convicts from the prison and all the animals. She's angry about the way other ferals have treated her and her ancestors, so this is her revenge." He took a deep breath. "She's going to create a feral army all of her own."

Glum landed beside Caw. *It would be like a new Dark Summer.*

Worse, said Screech, flapping in panic. *Every death would let her create a new feral to join her cause.*

With the stone, she would be unstoppable, added Shimmer.

"Well, she can't," said Selina. "We've got it, and all we have to do is make sure she can never find it."

Caw nodded, and looked to Bootlace. "We should hide it down here."

"What?" said Bootlace. "No, no, no. I looked after it for your mother, but..."

"Exactly," said Caw. "She trusted you, and you kept it safe. I bet the Mother of Flies doesn't even know about you. And even if she does, she'd never be able to find this place."

"Oh, I don't know about that," said a familiar voice.

Everyone turned to the cavern wall. The rock seemed to splinter into tiny fragments as hundreds of moths twitched their wings. They settled again, revealing the shape of Mr Silk, camouflaged against the rock. He held his gun at his hip, pointing it at Caw.

The crows jumped into the air with a flurry of beating wings, while the worms shrank away into the ground.

Then a squeaking horde of rats came rushing from the door, with Pinkerton skulking after them.

His mouth dry, Caw looked around desperately for another exit. But there was nowhere to run.

Chapter 17

"**Y**ou brought them here!" shouted Bootlace. "To my home!"

"How did you find us?" said Caw. He felt the weight of the stone in his pocket.

"How do you think, crow talker?" said Mr Silk. "Her children are everywhere. There is nowhere you can hide now."

Caw drew a deep breath and summoned his crows. *If* they could sense him from so deep underground. He searched for their black shadows in the ether, but they were faint.

"Give me the stone," said Mr Silk. He swivelled the gun to point at Lydia. "I know your weak spots, remember."

"He doesn't have it!" said Lydia defiantly. "We've hidden it."

Mr Silk laughed. "Is that so, my dear? Then why is his hand covering his pocket like that?"

Caw drew it back. *Come to me!* he willed his crows.

The gun went off with a crack, the barrel flaring in the gloom. Lydia leapt and screamed as a bullet ricocheted off the rock beside her.

"Don't test my patience," said Mr Silk.

Caw could feel them now. Their massed feathers and sharp beaks and shrieking voices. The flood of bodies coming through the grave door.

Caw's eyes went to the entranceway, where the rat feral stood oblivious. Silently he commanded his crows to plough through her.

"Shut the door, if you will," said Mr Silk.

Pinkerton looked startled. "The w-w-what?"

"The door, my good lady. Quickly, now."

The crows swept down the steps, hundreds of them, propelling themselves along the passage in an unstoppable wave.

Pinkerton slammed the door. Caw's heart sank as a succession of thuds sounded from the other side.

"Th-th-think you can outsmart a rat?" she said.

Her creatures swept towards Caw, and Glum and Screech landed at his feet, their bodies right in the rodents' path.

Where's Shim—? began Screech, before the rats swamped him.

Mr Silk cried out as Shimmer swooped on him, the gun going off in his hand. Caw heard a bullet ping off the roof of the cavern, and the gun hit the ground. Shimmer shrieked as she clung on to the moth feral's wrist, pecking and gouging. Blood splattered from his hand.

"Hide!" Caw yelled to the others.

Lydia and Selina ran, leaping through the carpet of rats. Caw saw the air move as a cloud of moths coalesced and dived towards their master. Shimmer was coated from beak to tail, and lost her grip, collapsing to the cave floor.

Caw ran for the gun, but Mr Silk knelt quickly and snatched it up. Caw saw the barrel turn to face him. "Don't despair, crow talker," said Mr Silk, leering cruelly. "This won't be the end of your line, I promise. She'll find some murderer or thief worthy to take charge of the crows."

He pulled the trigger just as a shape leapt across in front of Caw. Bootlace! The worm feral's body jerked with the impact of the shot. Mr Silk fired again, and Bootlace was driven back a step, but remained standing. Caw couldn't see any wounds at all – it was as if his body had just absorbed the bullets.

"If only it were that easy," said the worm feral with a grotesque smile.

Mr Silk looked at the gun in confusion, then fired three more shots at point blank range, before staggering as the ground at his feet broke apart. His foot slipped into a hole as worms broke through. "What the..." he said.

Caw turned, looking for Glum and Screech. Both

were pinned, their wings jerking at strange angles as they tried to break free of the rats. Caw kicked one of the rodents aside, then grabbed another by its tail and tossed it. More squirmed up his legs, biting as they went. He fought his panic as he saw Pinkerton hopping up on to a rock, laughing maniacally.

Caw looked up to see Mr Silk finally drag his leg free of the cloying earth and club Bootlace fiercely across the jaw. The worm feral fell to the ground with a grunt.

Shaking off the rats that were clawing up his body, Caw charged at the moth feral, reaching for the gun as Mr Silk brought it round again. They slammed into the wall together. Teeth gritted, Caw smashed the moth feral's arms against the rock until he dropped the gun. Caw bent hastily to grab it. *Oof!* He felt a knee driven into his stomach and crumpled, gasping for breath, the gun out of his reach.

Shimmer had managed to scramble free of the moth swarm. She flew over to the gun, hooking her talons around the barrel and pushing herself off the ground, dropping the weapon well clear of the moth feral.

Mr Silk threw his weight over Caw's body, hands searching in his pockets. Caw struggled, but the shock of the blow had made him weak. He knew as soon as the moth feral rolled off him that he had lost the Midnight Stone.

"I've got it, Pinkerton!" shouted Mr Silk.

The rat feral jumped down from her boulder. Caw

wheezed, unable to move. He could see Selina hiding behind one of the tombs, but where was Lydia? Bootlace was groaning, trying to stand as rats clambered over him.

Mr Silk was transfixed by the stone glinting in his hand.

"Don't seem much, does it?" he said. He pocketed the stone, then his face turned nasty. He kicked Caw in the gut again, throwing him on to his back.

Through the pain, Caw saw Lydia at last. She was moving towards the door, with a finger placed on her lips. What was she up to?

"Time to smash this crow's brains in," said Mr Silk. He knelt, picking up a rock the size of a football and hoisting it over his head. "Goodbye, crow talker."

Caw heard the door thump open and Mr Silk's eyes flicked sideways. A split second later he was overwhelmed by a black cloud of crows. Through the flapping wings, Caw saw his arms give way and the rock fall to the ground.

Caw rolled on to his front, gasping. He could hardly see, so alive was the air with insects and birds. Crows veered wildly as the moths assaulted them in swarms. Many of the birds flew straight into the walls, disorientated by the insect plague.

He spotted Bootlace crawling along the ground, dozens of rodents covering his body. The worm feral climbed unsteadily to his feet and advanced on Pinkerton.

"Caw, it's time to fulfil your promise," said Bootlace. "I think I'll take this rat feral with me."

For a moment Caw wasn't sure what he meant, but then he remembered their deal.

He glanced around, but couldn't see the Crow's Beak.

"Here, Caw!" cried Selina, picking the blade up from the floor where it had fallen. Drawing back her arm, she sent it spinning across the cavern. Caw caught it by the hilt and lifted the point of the blade. The sword thrummed in his hand, as if charged with an electric current. As Caw brought it down in a vertical swipe, he felt the air resist softly, like water. The blade opened a rip of pure blinding light in front of him. The rift widened. Rats and crows shrieked as one, backing away. Pinkerton shielded her eyes.

Blinking, Caw saw Bootlace's face, open-mouthed, his eyes filmed with tears. "It's beautiful!" he cried.

The worm feral ran at Pinkerton, his gaze fixed on the doorway to the Land of the Dead. He wrapped his arms around the rat feral's waist and dived headlong. Pinkerton screamed as he bundled her into the portal. Then the light swallowed them both, cutting off her cry midway. The rift shrank, its edges pulling together like a healing wound. As the last point of light vanished, a gust of wind swept across the cave, extinguishing most of the candles and leaving them in semi-darkness.

A silence settled through the cave as Caw stared at

the Crow's Beak in his hand. It felt cold and lifeless once more. The Land of the Dead had left a scattering of fine ash over the blade.

Selina was pale with shock. "Where are Bootlace and Pinkerton?"

"Dead," said Caw.

"Just like that?" said Selina.

Caw nodded.

"More importantly though, where are Mr Silk and the Midnight Stone?" said Lydia.

Caw looked to where Mr Silk had been brought down by the crows, but his heart plummeted. He had gone. Crows landed on the ground beside their injured comrades, but there wasn't a single living moth to be seen. The gun was missing too.

"Where did he go?" said Caw.

Lydia shook her head. "I was watching the portal," she said.

Quickly Caw crossed the cavern to the spot where Mr Silk had fallen. There was a pool of blood, then a trail of thick drops. He followed them towards the door.

He must have slipped out, said Glum.

Caw was relieved at least to see the old crow unharmed apart from a few jutting feathers. Screech was limping beside him on his broken leg and Shimmer's beak held a twitching moth. She tossed her head back and swallowed it.

"It's over then," said Selina. "We've lost it."

Caw looked around at the devastation. The worm feral's home suddenly seemed more like a crypt than ever. Silent, dark, a place of stillness. Strewn with corpses, the air thick with the essence of lives lost. And though he still stood, Caw knew he was on the vanquished side. For four hundred years, the crow line had protected the Midnight Stone and now he had let it go. Not only that, but the Mother of Flies now knew exactly what it could do and planned to use it for evil.

Caw fought the despair that threatened to cripple him. Hardening his heart, he sheathed the Crow's Beak and strode towards the door. His crows fluttered behind him.

"We'll have to hurry," said Lydia. "If we don't catch Mr Silk soon, he'll give her the stone. She already has the convicts and the animals to create her own feral army."

Caw nodded. The words of Black Corvus wouldn't leave his head – the promise of the crow line. *We will protect it to our dying breaths.* "Well then," he said. "We'd better get after him."

Chapter 18

When Caw and his companions emerged, the clouds above the graveyard were thicker even than before – swollen a deep and ominous indigo against the night sky. His crows surged from the ground in an inky torrent, settling across the graveyard again, an army exhausted by battle. Many carried broken wings, or bled on to the pale stones. A few rats scurried out as well, aimless and confused now that their pure animal natures had returned. Caw wondered if there would ever be another feral to guide them and whether he or she would use them for good or for evil.

There was no sign of the moth feral. "Shimmer – take a few crows, get up there and look for Mr Silk," said Caw. "He can't have gone far."

The wiry crow flapped away, followed by several others. They fanned out across the sky, heading in the direction of the city.

Caw heaved the tombstone back into place, sealing the worm feral's home. Then, closing his eyes, he drew his crows to him. Those in the graveyard cracked their wings and launched from their perches, and more still came in waves from the sky. "Get ready to fly," Caw told Selina and Lydia.

Lydia lifted her arms, and Selina followed suit. The crows took up their positions, clinging on to the girls' clothing, their bodies jostling. Caw's heart swelled with pride. Even against the odds they faced, and reeling from the battles already fought, the silent loyalty of the crows was absolute.

Glum and Screech gripped his own shoulders.

"Not you, Screech," said Caw. "You need to rest that leg."

It's fine, said Screech, with a fierceness that brooked no argument. *Let's go get 'em!*

Once more into the breach, said Glum.

As his feet left the ground, Caw felt the first drop of rain fall; a fat, warm splash on his skin. Shimmer came circling back. *He's in a white car!* she said. *Heading back towards the city.*

"Lead the way," said Caw.

With a rip of thunder, the sky released its deluge. Caw hardly noticed as the crows rose in jerks, over the graves, then up as high as the steeple. Wind made Caw's body sway in their grip, and Blackstone became an indistinct blur of smeared light and silhouetted buildings through the steel rods of rain. Caw looked at his companions, already sodden, and saw their faces set with determination.

Shimmer flew in front, and the three of them followed in the grip of the birds. It wasn't long before Caw saw a pale car speeding along a winding road below. It had to be Mr Silk. It was some sort of old-fashioned vehicle, with a growling engine; completely white with huge chrome fenders. Its headlights shone golden streaks on the slick tarmac.

Caw didn't know what to do. The car was moving too fast for him to drop down on the bonnet, as he had when he'd rescued Quaker.

Tunnel ahead! said Screech.

Caw looked up and saw they were heading for a dark mouth as the road entered a low hillside. The crows began to lift him higher, to carry him over the top of the tunnel entrance.

"No!" he said. "Keep on his tail!"

They dipped again, while those carrying Lydia and Selina continued to rise out of harm's way, above the hill. The car shot inside. Caw willed a cluster of crows to follow with him. They swept him into the strobe-lit tunnel, his feet barely a metre above the road surface.

"Get in his path!" he shouted. "Distract him!"

The crows who weren't carrying Caw accelerated past

him, sweeping towards the car. Caw saw the reflection of Mr Silk's face in the wing mirror watching him, and with a roar the vehicle speeded up.

But the crows were faster. Inch by inch they overtook the car, then closed formation in front of it, blotting out the moth feral's view.

Caw heard the blare of a horn and his eyes filled with light. The crows jerked him sideways as another car whipped past in the opposite direction. His heart was thudding like a jackhammer.

Mr Silk tried to outmanoeuvre the crows, veering left and right in the tunnel to find clear road. Caw willed the birds to close in on the windscreen. The car's front wheel locked with a sudden screech of brakes, streaming smoke. Its rear end slid out as if on ice and slammed into the central barrier, and a window pane exploded outwards on the driver's side. Caw told his crows to bring him level as the car straightened and accelerated once more.

As he drew alongside, Caw saw Mr Silk gripping the wheel in both hands, peering over the top to try to see the road through the barrier of birds. He looked right and his eyes locked on to Caw. Then he reached down, bringing up his gun.

Bang! Bang!

Two shots cracked from the barrel and Caw twisted away. The crows lagged back, hauling him out of range.

They were reaching the end of the tunnel, where the road emerged again. Caw let the car go first, following through the downpour and out into the city. There were more cars here, and Lydia and Selina were waiting suspended beneath their crows.

"We've got to stop him!" Caw shouted.

The three of them swung through the sky as Mr Silk's car threaded through the traffic at speed, mounting kerbs and throwing up spray. It bounced over a traffic island and a hubcap spun off one of the wheels. Horns blared up and down the street. Caw couldn't stay hidden – he only hoped the weather would conceal him from the normal citizens of Blackstone.

Mr Silk reached a set of red lights and didn't slow. Behind him several cars smashed into each others' paths with sickening crunches. They were travelling alongside the river now. Across on the opposite bank rose the buildings of the financial district and the apartment where the Mother of Flies lurked with her army-in-waiting. If the moth feral reached it, the chase was over.

The car skidded around a corner and on to a bridge. There was only one thing for it. Caw swooped forward, positioning himself over the roof of the car. He was just about to drop when a single black shape darted down in front of him.

With perfect timing, Shimmer dived through the open car window, straight at the moth feral. Caw couldn't see what was happening inside, but he heard Mr Silk's cries. The vehicle jerked, first one way, then the other. The moth feral lost control completely and the back end spun a half-circle. It hit the crash barrier at the edge of the bridge, and bounced off. The wheels on the right side left the road.

Shimmer! cried Screech, as the car flipped over.

With a horrible squeal of grinding metal, the car slid along on its roof, showering sparks. Wheels spinning, it smashed into the barrier on the opposite side, buckling the metal railings there and sliding over the edge. Broken glass scattered into the river below as the car lodged, upside-down, half suspended over the water.

Caw's crows swooped lower at his command and he dropped the last six feet to the ground, running to the stricken vehicle. It wobbled precariously over the drop. Oil was dripping from a puncture in the tank and the smell of burning rubber filled Caw's nostrils.

From inside, he heard someone groaning.

Cars on the road were slowing down. Caw heard someone say, "Call the cops!"

Shimmer flapped out of the broken window and hopped across the underside of the car. *He's all yours,* she said.

That was incredible! said Screech. *You stopped him single-wingedly!*

Caw edged closer to the broken crash railings. The

door of the car swung open over the drop and a bloodied hand emerged. Caw saw Mr Silk's face was bruised by the crash. Moths fluttered anxiously across his crumpled suit. He sagged forward, hanging out of the car, but his seatbelt held him firm. His eyes found Caw.

"Crow talker!" he growled.

"Give me the stone," said Caw.

"I don't think so," said Mr Silk. He reached across his body, and Caw readied himself to duck in case it was a gun. But he heard only a click as the seat belt released. Mr Silk clambered to the edge of the door. And at the same moment, the car tipped.

The moth feral leapt for the edge of the bridge with a cry of terror as the car groaned and then slid out over the drop. He just managed to hold on to a piece of the crash barrier as the vehicle plummeted into the river with a tremendous splash. It floated a few metres in the current, then disappeared out of sight.

Caw heard car doors slamming as people exited their vehicles. Then Selina's voice. "Stay back! It's not safe!"

Mr Silk's features writhed in fear as he hung over the water. He gritted his teeth and pulled, but his arms weren't strong enough to heave himself over the edge to safety. "Don't let me drown!" he said.

Caw knelt over him. "Give me the stone and I'll help you up."

Mr Silk clenched his eyes shut, as if trying not to think about the river swirling below.

"I promise I won't let you fall," said Caw, "but you have to give me the stone."

He held out his arm.

Mr Silk opened his eyes again. "It's in my pocket," he said. "I can't give it to you without letting go."

Lydia had arrived at Caw's side. "Don't trust him," she said.

"Please!" said Mr Silk. "I give you my word as a gentleman."

His fingers were slipping.

Caw reached down and grabbed the moth feral's left arm with both hands. "I've got you!" he said. He braced himself to take Mr Silk's weight.

"Pull me up!"

"The stone first," said Lydia. "Use your other hand."

"Quickly!" said Caw. "I can't hold you for long!"

Mr Silk's right hand rooted in his pocket, and he took out the Midnight Stone. At the same moment, the moths lifted away from him like a shadow and flew away. He watched them go, face twitching in terror.

"Here!" he said. "Take it!"

As he reached up, a single black spot landed on his hand. Lydia was leaning over the edge to take the stone, but Mr Silk paused. "No..." he muttered. "Oh no!"

The air filled with buzzing, and more flies swarmed over his hand and arm.

"No, please!" he shouted, flailing. With each jerking movement, Caw's grip loosened.

Flies spread across Mr Silk's body, piling on top of one another in a solid bulk. Then, before Caw's eyes, they became Cynthia Davenport. She was hanging on to the moth feral's back, wrapping her limbs around him. Caw's arms screamed with the extra weight.

"Hello, Mr Silk," she said, leaning close to his ear. "I believe you have something for me?"

She reached along his arm and prised his fingers from the Midnight Stone. He was cringing in fear, his eyes clenched tight.

"I didn't mean to..." he said. "I was going to bring it to you, I promise."

Caw couldn't hold on any longer. His fingers slipped off Mr Silk's sleeve, and at the same moment, the Mother of Flies transformed back into her insects. Her swarm seemed to hold the moth feral, suspended in the air.

"No, you weren't," whispered her voice. The cloud of flies turned its head towards Caw. "Act wisely, crow talker. Run from Blackstone while you have the chance."

Her swarm exploded from Mr Silk's body and his eyes opened wide. He fell with a scream, his body disappearing into the river, as the swarm of flies dissolved into the night.

Chapter 19

Caw's blood coursed hot as they approached the financial district, despite the cold of the whipping gales and his saturated clothes. The crows shared his desperation and his anger – he could sense it, the power of their wings flowing through him as they cut through the wind and soared towards the tall tower where Cynthia Davenport lived.

"She'll be waiting for us!" shouted Selina. She hung from the crows, her hair matted to her head.

"Who cares?" said Lydia, hood pulled up as she flew on the other side of Caw.

"I'm only saying," Selina replied. "We can't just storm in."

"Easy for you to say," snapped Lydia. "But my parents are in there."

Caw tried to block out their bickering. The memories of the worm feral were still fresh. All those men and women in that fire-lit study had put their faith in Black Corvus, and for three hundred years the crow line had not let them down. That wasn't going to change today. All that history meant nothing if he failed.

But the Midnight Stone was already in Cynthia Davenport's grasp. Back then, the ferals had been fighting the superstitions of humans. They couldn't have known that one day their deadliest enemy would be among their own number.

Had she already put her plan into action? Was she at this moment creating new lines of ferals?

Caw willed his crows to slow and the ones carrying the girls drew close.

"Selina's right," he said. "Let's set down in the courtyard."

He didn't wait for Lydia to argue. The crows circled around the blind side of the building as sheet lighting flashed in the bruised bellies of the clouds. Their flight followed a gently descending path until Caw's feet bumped against the ground. The tower rose above them, the windows gleaming black; a dark, thrusting silhouette.

"Stay close," Caw told the crows, as they set down Lydia and Selina too. "I'll need you again soon."

The birds fell across a garden of ornamental trees, blackening the branches. Only Screech, Shimmer and Glum remained with him.

Caw led his friends towards the front of the building

and crouched behind Cynthia Davenport's limo. The ground was littered with shards of glass from the broken window he had leapt through earlier.

"What's the plan?" asked Selina. "I guess the elevator is out of the question?"

Caw noticed something moving in the forecourt – two small foxes, nosing around in some bushes. Mr Silk had been wrong when he said they wouldn't come – Mrs Strickham had loyal creatures, even here.

Caw stared up – from this angle, he couldn't see the apartment at all. There was definitely a faint glow at the top of the building though. But it was seventy floors up and her flies would surely be on the lookout. The others were looking at him, expectant. *They're relying on me. I brought them here, but for what?* He couldn't let them go up there too. This wasn't their fight – both had been dragged in through no fault of their own, just because of who their parents were.

"I'll go up there alone," he said. He moved away.

"No!" said Lydia, grabbing his arm. "Don't even think about it!"

"We're coming with you," said Selina.

"You can't," he pleaded. "This is a fight for ferals."

"No it isn't," said Lydia. "Can't you see that? If the Mother of Flies wins, she won't stop at wiping out the other ferals. She'll take over the whole city. Everyone will suffer."

Caw tried to pull his arm out of the way, but Lydia gripped it harder.

"You've got to let us help," said Selina.

Caw didn't want to fight them, but he hardened his heart. "OK," he said. "You're right."

Lydia let go of him and they both lifted their arms expectantly.

You can't let them come, said Glum, as if reading his thoughts. *They'll get themselves killed.*

"Get ready," Caw said, as crows flocked across their bodies. He hated lying, but Lydia and Selina had their whole lives ahead of them. Black Corvus had made a promise that he intended to keep himself.

He told his crows to lift him, and him alone. And as he rose into the air, those on the girls detached themselves.

"Caw, no!" said Lydia. "Don't you dare leave me here!"

"You need us!" said Selina. They both glared up at him.

"If I don't come back, you have to run away," he said. "Blackstone won't be safe."

"Shut up, Caw!" shouted Lydia. "We're supposed to be friends!"

"We are!" he called back.

Their shouts faded as the crows lifted him away.

You did the right thing, said Glum as they rose higher and higher.

Yep, said Shimmer. *So what's the plan?*

Caw fished around for something to say.

Let me guess, said Screech. *Dive headlong into almost certain death?*

"That's about it," said Caw. His arteries pumped with adrenaline, making his skin tingle.

Pah! said Shimmer. *Plans are overrated.*

"I won't hold it against you if you want to stay behind," said Caw. "After everything you've done..."

I'm pretty sure you would, said Glum. *Without us, you'd be left to gravity.*

Caw couldn't help but smile, despite everything. He knew the crows weren't going anywhere. They never had and they never would.

The windows of the building reeled past and his blurred reflection streamed across them as they climbed. Whatever awaited him, however afraid he was, he would face it without turning away, just as his mother had faced the Spinning Man. He'd make her proud. Crumb too. And even if he died, at least he'd done all in his power to stop the Mother of Flies. The crow line would have held firm, and if their spirits lingered in the Land of the Dead, they would nod and say he had done his duty.

Caw's heart surged at the thought of his ancestors and the crows lifted him faster through the air. He flew as close to the building's side as possible, trying to stay out of sight. As he reached the broken apartment window, he saw the lights inside were off. He let the crows carry him inside, over the bullet-riddled furniture and broken glass. Panic rose in his chest. He hadn't thought that the Mother of Flies might actually go somewhere else to carry out her plan.

But as he emerged into the night again, he realised he could hear voices from above. They climbed higher. Now he saw the source of the light – from the roof, angled spotlights were illuminating columns of golden rain. Between them, a helicopter stood perched on an elevated platform. Caw told the crows to carry him behind it and they obeyed. As soon as his feet touched down, he waved a hand and they dropped back out of sight over the roof's edge. He crouched, peering around the edge of the helicopter.

A fire door was open, and Cynthia Davenport stood beside it, wearing a black coat and leather gloves, smiling triumphantly as the line of convicts emerged. The first was Lugmann. He clutched a lead, the other end attached by a collar to the black panther Caw had seen caged inside. The creature prowled lazily, muzzled but compliant, into the rain.

Next came a tall, gangling dark-skinned man with a beard. He held a glass jar, stuffed with a large, coiled centipede. Caw felt a flash of anger at seeing Emily's creature imprisoned so soon after her death.

More convicts followed. A grey-haired stocky man of

middle age led a monkey on a leash. The creature was howling and tugging back, but the convict yanked him on.

"Quicker!" said the Mother of Flies impatiently. "Form a circle."

One by one, the former prisoners came out, each with an animal of their own. Birds on tethers, insects in containers, primates and dogs wheeled in their crates and cages from the hidden room in the apartment below. At one point a thug with several piercings in his eyebrows, nose and lips came out backwards. He was carrying one side of a stretcher. Sprawled across it, unconscious, was the brown bear. Caw realised that it had probably come from the zoo. Did that mean the Mother of Flies had the other creatures, too, somewhere – deadly species likes tigers and crocodiles and wolverines? If they were let loose on the streets of Blackstone... it was too horrible to think about.

The other side of the bear's stretcher was carried by a man with a snake wrapped around his forearm. They took positions in a loose circle on the roof beside the helicopter. The animals snarled and snapped as the rain bucketed down.

Last of all came Mr and Mrs Strickham, hands and ankles tied together with cord, making them stumble awkwardly. A scrawny convict in a baggy prison shirt followed them with a gun.

Cynthia Davenport strode into the centre of the circle of prisoners and animals. They were all talking to each other and laughing.

"On your knees," growled the wiry man, pointing the gun at Velma Strickham.

When she didn't obey, he kicked Mr Strickham in the back of the legs. Lydia's father crumpled with a cry, dragging down his wife with him.

"Leave him alone!" shouted Lydia's mother.

The convict laughed. "Or what? When all this is over and you and your line are dead, maybe I'll be the new fox feral. How about that?"

Caw shuddered. That was Lydia the man was threatening, not just Mrs Strickham. It suddenly became clear to him. No feral was safe. All the prisoners from the zoo ambush... sooner or later the Mother of Flies would kill them all, extinguishing their lines so that she could resurrect them under her own control. Pip and Crumb... All who could stand in her way.

"You first!" said the Mother of Flies, pointing a gloved finger at the man with the beard. "Come to me."

The man came forward uncertainly. He looked scared, Caw thought.

The Mother of Flies took the Midnight Stone from her pocket. Caw's skin prickled at the sight of it.

"Hold out your hand," she ordered.

"Will it hurt?" the man asked.

Her lip turned up in disgust. "I'm about to give you and your wretched descendants a destiny greater than anything you could ever have hoped for. Now give me your hand!"

The man flinched as if she'd slapped him, and did as he was told. Mrs Strickham placed the stone in his palm. Caw saw that the assembled convicts had gone quiet.

"Now, take your gift," she said. "Touch the creature."

He crouched, placed the jar on the roof, then reached inside. At the moment his fingers touched the squirming centipede, his body jerked as if shocked with an electric current and the stone flashed white. Caw felt something pass through his own body too, soft as a summer breeze.

The convict fell backwards, breaking contact. But the air still fizzed with unseen energy, an echo of the ancient power contained within the stone. The animals in the cages all cowered into silence. Then the convict shook his head to clear it; he looked at the jar and frowned. The centipede moved slowly, climbed out down the side, and disappeared into the cuff of his sleeve. It emerged at his collar, creeping around his neck.

He stood up, grinning widely.

The circle broke into cheers and whoops as he rejoined them. Velma Strickham bowed her head in defeat. Her husband looked sickened.

Caw looked on hopelessly.

"Next!" said Cynthia Davenport.

A teenage girl with greasy locks came forward with a golden eagle on her gloved hand. She could barely lift the huge bird.

As she took her place beside the stone, a dog started barking furiously in Caw's direction. He ducked out of sight behind the helicopter. What could he do? Send a barrage of crows to try and get the stone? No – they wouldn't get close. Another gasp from the assembled convicts told him the eagle and the girl had bonded. Caw still had the Crow's Beak. But if any of them had guns...

He sat motionless, paralysed with fear, as more and more convicts were united with creatures, one after another.

"Next!" shouted the Mother of Flies. "You!"

Caw peered over the landing pad again, just in time to see Lugmann with the muzzled panther. He held out his fingers tentatively and the panther swiped at him with a paw. The convict backed away with a grunt.

"Get on with it!" said Cynthia Davenport. "Make it yours, you coward."

Lugmann reached out to touch the panther's shoulder and the light flashed again.

Something tickled Caw's hand and he looked down to see a single fly crawling along his wrist.

"I think we have an uninvited guest," said the Mother of Flies.

There was no point staying hidden any more. Caw stepped out into the open.

As she turned to face him, so did all the convicts, and the Strickhams.

"Caw!" Lydia's mother yelled. "Go! Fly away! It's over!"

The convicts all wore bemused expressions and glanced at Cynthia Davenport uncertainly.

She looked utterly untroubled. "Crows are stubborn creatures, aren't they?" she said.

The convicts all laughed, but Caw stood his ground. He felt the crows waiting and called more. He sensed their gathering strength. When the moment came, he would unleash their fury.

"That stone belongs to my family," Caw said, struggling to keep his voice level. "I've come to get it back."

The Mother of Flies smiled. "No, you haven't, crow talker," she said. "You've come to witness my triumph."

Chapter 20

The convicts began to break from their circle, approaching Caw. The panther beside Lugmann had lost its muzzle and its white fangs glistened.

"Caw!" pleaded Mrs Strickham. "Look after Lydia! That's all that matters now."

The Mother of Flies shook her head. "Don't worry, Caw," she said. "Once you're dead, I'll find someone suitable to fill your shoes."

Caw stepped back as the convicts advanced in a line, their animals hopping, scuttling, prowling and flapping at their sides.

"Hey, what about me!" said the pierced man beside the bear. "I haven't got my powers yet!"

"You can wait," said the Mother of Flies, slipping the Midnight Stone into her pocket. "How does it feel, Caw?" she asked. "You crows always thought you were the greatest of all ferals. I wonder what the mighty Black Corvus would have made of you."

Caw remembered his ancestor's face, and the way the others had looked to him for guidance.

"I don't know," he said. "But he'd have hated you and everything you stand for. He wanted to protect the ferals, not use their powers for his own gain."

"Is that right?" asked the Mother of Flies. "He never protected *my* ancestors. No one did. That's why I had to make my own allies. New ferals, who understand that the fly line is to be honoured, not scorned."

"You're just a criminal like any other," shouted Mr Strickham.

The Mother of Flies turned on him angrily. "Can any criminal do this?"

She flung a hand at him and flies swarmed across the rooftop in a black ball, enveloping his head in a mask of bristling bodies. Caw heard muffled screams as Mr Strickham felt forward, writhing on the ground.

"Stop!" said Mrs Strickham. Cynthia Davenport lifted her hand and the flies buzzed away, as Lydia's father gasped for air. "Just teaching your husband some manners," she said. "There'll be time to deal with all my enemies, soon enough. Why rush?"

The convicts were slowly forming a semicircle around Caw. They looked hungry for blood.

"So," said the Mother of Flies. "What are you waiting for? Use your powers!"

The bearded man plucked the centipede from his neck and dropped it to the ground. The creature unfurled to a length of nearly two feet and scurried towards Caw.

Caw barely had to think before Glum darted down from the sky. He scooped the centipede up in his talons and carried it away, squirming.

The girl launched her eagle. Its wings spread majestically, six feet wide at least, feathers speckled white on their underside. With a piercing screech it swooped at Caw, its talons bent to tear at his face. He ducked in panic, throwing an arm over his head, and felt the claws sink easily through his jacket sleeve and into his flesh. The pain made him cry out, but he wriggled free.

The next moment his face was full of flapping, shrieking eagle, the beak stabbing like a dagger. Caw managed to hurl his jacket over its head, and the bird let go, rising away blindly on powerful wings, trying to shake off the cover and rapidly tearing it apart. Caw threw out a bleeding arm and crows smacked into the partly covered bird of prey. The noise was horrible as the birds attacked en masse. Feathers rained down, both black and brown. The scrapping birds hit the rooftop and more crows piled on. The giant bird began to move more weakly as the crows attacked relentlessly.

Caw tore his gaze away as he heard a low growl. His blood froze as he saw the snarling panther leap forwards. Crows flew bravely into its path, but were knocked aside with ease. Shimmer managed to get her talons into its back. The cat didn't even slow and she tumbled off. Caw saw another crow snatched in its jaws. The panther tossed it aside with a vicious jerk of its head.

Caw backed off quickly, palms sweating, and only stopped when he reached the roof's edge. Fear paralysed him on the spot as the panther closed in. This was it – there was nowhere to go.

The panther pounced and Caw leapt up at the same time. He used his fear, channelling it through his body, willing his body to change into its crow form. The pain of the transformation, sudden and powerful, snatched his breath away. He rose on crow wings above the diving cat, leaving nothing in its path. Caw looked behind to see a whirl of flailing limbs and gnashing teeth, then the panther's eyes widening with terror as it plummeted, spinning, towards the unforgiving ground far below.

A hand swatted Caw's wing, turning him over, then yanked him from the sky. He hit the wet rooftop and at once his hold on his crow form began to loosen and his limbs became human once more. Lugmann was holding his arm, anger twisting his face. "I'll make you pay for that!" he said, spitting.

Blows rained down from all sides as the other

convicts surrounded him. Caw curled into a ball, unable to tell where all the different stabs of pain were coming from. He saw boots and swinging legs, but couldn't do a thing to stop them. He tried to call the crows, but his mind wouldn't focus. All around, from their cages, the other animals filled the air with their cries. Caw tasted blood in his mouth from a split lip. A fist connected with his ear and his head spun.

"Get off him!" yelled a distant voice. "Now!"

A few more punches connected, but the bodies around Caw began to separate. Weakly, he rolled over, and finally managed to call his crows. *Help me...*

None came.

As the convicts moved back, Caw saw why. Across the rooftop and in the sky, clumps of flies swarmed over every one of his birds. He caught glimpses of beaks and wings as they struggled to break free.

Cynthia Davenport was covered too, from her boots right up to the base of her chin. Caw couldn't see even a millimetre of her clothing. Flies coated her hair. Only her face remained untouched by the insects. She lifted her arms and as she did so her body lifted from the ground. They were *carrying* her. She drifted like a black spectre across the rooftop towards him.

"It's over, Caw," she said, floating in mid-air.

Caw managed to prop himself up on his elbows, his body throbbing with pain. His arm was gouged from the eagle attack and he felt blood streaming from both nostrils. Something was wrong with his side, making it hard to draw breath – a broken rib, perhaps.

"Your mother would be ashamed to see you now," said the Mother of Flies, hovering. "For so many generations the crow talkers kept the stone a secret, but there was always going to be one weak link – a feral who let down his line. That's you, Jack Carmichael. The time of the crows is over. It is time for the flies to take the throne."

"There's no throne!" said Caw. "You're nothing but a plague – you *and* your flies."

"I've heard it all before, crow talker," said Cynthia Davenport. "Filthy. Repulsive. Unclean. That's what they called my mother. That's what they've always called us. But flies are survivors. My army will hunt the old order for sport. And even when the fly line is avenged, and this city is dead, my children will feed from its corpse and grow stronger."

"And then?" said Caw, grimacing as he shifted again. "You're no different from the Spinning Man. You just want power no matter what it costs. Who wants to rule over a dead city?"

"I'm *nothing* like the Spinning Man," said the Mother of Flies. Lightning forked above. "He was an arrogant fool who let himself be bettered twice. I crawled my way up from the bottom. I've fought for everything I've ever had, and I've come out stronger than he ever was. Stronger than he ever could have been."

Caw made up his mind. If he was going to die, he would do so defiantly. "If you say so, but I think spiders will always be greater than flies. Your precious creatures die in their webs, don't they?"

A flicker of pain crossed Cynthia Davenport's face. Her flies set her down and buzzed away in a black wave. She reached inside her jacket and pulled out a gun. "Time for your gift to pass to someone more worthy," she said, pointing the gun at his head. "I'll do you the honour of making it quick. The Land of the Dead awaits you, crow talker."

Caw closed his eyes.

Chapter 21

Bang!

It took a split-second for Caw to realise the noise wasn't a gun.

His eyes shot open and he saw that the Mother of Flies was looking behind her, where the door to the stairwell had swung open, hitting the wall hard. Selina stood there, breathing heavily.

"I won't let you do this," she said.

"You think you can stop me?" sneered her mother. "A child? Your heart was always soft. You'll never be worthy of my power."

"I don't want anything from you!" said Selina. "And it's not me who's going to stop you." She jerked a thumb over her shoulder. "It's them!"

Dozens of foxes flooded through the door, snarling. Caw had never seen so many in one place before. Lydia came behind them, her cheeks pink with running.

The foxes leapt at the scrawny convict pointing the gun at their mistress, and he staggered backwards with a cry of terror. Then they set about savaging the bonds that tied Velma Strickham and her husband.

"Save Caw!" Lydia's mother commanded, and the rest of the foxes ran across the rooftop towards the convicts. The convicts panicked and backed away, trying to use each other as human shields. Others scattered, with foxes on their heels.

Caw's heart filled with hope.

"Cowards!" said the Mother of Flies. "They're only *foxes!*"

Several banks of flies swooped down from the sky. They swept across the rooftop, breaking into small swarms, each group headed for one of Velma Strickham's creatures.

The Mother of Flies was distracted now and Caw knew he wouldn't get another chance.

Standing sent shocks of pain across his body, but he found his feet and charged. Cynthia Davenport turned at the last moment. Caw ploughed into her, but the next moment she was gone, evaporating into a cloud of flies that filled his face. He fell in a heap and heard a click at his back. The Mother of Flies stood there, pointing the gun at him.

"No escape this time," she said. Her finger twitched on the trigger.

Selina leapt on to her mother's back with a cry, spinning the Mother of Flies around. The gun clattered to the ground and Caw dived for it, but a foot got there first, kicking the gun, skittering, across the rooftop. Caw looked up to see the pierced convict sneering at him. The man lifted a foot and Caw saw the ridges of the sole as it rose to stamp on his skull.

"Agh!" the convict wailed, as a barrage of black birds swept into him, knocking him off balance.

The Mother of Flies was spinning round, still trying to grab Selina, who was clinging to her back. "Get off me!" she yelled.

"You don't tell me what to do any more," said her daughter.

Cynthia Davenport collapsed to her knees, then her body crumbled into thousands of flies, leaving Selina breathing heavily on the ground. The Mother of Flies reappeared a few feet away, where the gun had come to rest. She picked it up, as Selina stepped in front of Caw.

The fly feral lowered the gun a fraction. "Out of the way!" she said.

"You'll have to shoot me first!" said Selina.

"Don't think I won't," said her mother, but Caw could see she was hesitating. *Come!* he willed. Any crow would do.

"Do it, then," said Selina. "I'd rather be dead than your daughter."

The Mother of Flies' face turned hard and she lifted the gun. "Very well," she said.

The barrel flared at the same moment that Screech dropped, talons first, on to Cynthia Davenport's arm. A bullet sparked on the ground in front of Selina's foot and her leg jerked from beneath her. She screamed and gripped her shin with one hand. Caw rushed to Selina's side. Blood oozed between her fingers. "She shot me!" she said, gritting her teeth.

Whoomp-whoomp-whoomp!

The helicopter was stirring into life. In the pilot's seat sat Lugmann and the others were piling into the back. Some had foxes hanging off their clothes, as they struggled into the already full chopper cabin. They'd left their animals behind, howling and clawing and scrambling in their cages. Velma Strickham and her husband had been driven back near the stairwell by swarms of flies, and the foxes were in disarray, tormented by insects.

Selina's mother shook her arm wildly, dropping the gun and throwing Screech off.

She looked at Caw and her daughter, then at the helicopter. "I'll deal with you later," she snapped at the fleeing convicts. She pulled her coat around her, then stopped, hand on her pocket, fear in her eyes. "Where is it?"

For a moment, Caw didn't understand, but then

Selina opened her bloodied hand to reveal the Midnight Stone. "Looking for this?" she said.

"How did you...?" muttered the Mother of Flies.

Caw knew how. Selina had taken it when she was on her mother's back.

"Give it to me!" howled Cynthia Davenport.

"Never!" said Selina. "All this time, you used me. You pretended to care. You used my love for you and twisted it for your own ends. Well, now I've got new friends who I really care about and you're not going to hurt them any more."

Caw stood up, stepping in front of Selina to face his enemy. He sensed his crows massing behind him and clenched his fists, summoning more. He let the tendrils of his power reach across the storm-tossed city and called all the crows in Blackstone.

"Look at that," he said, "your friends are all running away."

The Mother of Flies smiled at him. "I am never alone while I have my children." She closed her eyes and raised her arms into the sky. Lightning flashed again. Caw looked up and saw that the clouds above were almost entirely black though the rain seemed to have stopped.

Then with a sinking sensation Caw realised they weren't clouds at all – they were flies. Millions and millions of flies, in a boiling, swirling swarm. And it hadn't stopped raining – they were clustering so heavily overhead that the downpour was no longer reaching the rooftop.

"See, crow talker!" cried the Mother of Flies. "You still have a lot to learn."

Caw glanced back and saw foxes running for the cover of the stairwell, where Lydia and her father were lying on the ground, hands shielding their heads. Mrs Strickham tried to stand, but the tempest of flies drove her to her knees. Selina was half-walking, half-crawling, dragging her injured leg, towards the fire escape.

The helicopter lifted slowly, its rotors whipping the Mother of Flies' hair across her face. Then it banked away, climbing into the sky until it looked like a distant insect itself and thunder drowned the chopping of its rotors.

Cynthia Davenport threw out an arm towards Caw and it stretched, dissolving into flies that swarmed towards his face. As the insects enveloped his head, Caw clamped his eyes closed, focusing all his powers inward, then sprang off the rooftop as a crow. Opening his wings, he let a gust carry him thirty feet into the air. The Mother of Flies watched him with a smile, then exploded into her insect form. She climbed after him, still in the shape of a woman.

Caw sent his crows to take her on, and they shot towards her body-swarm with beaks open, snapping up flies. She broke apart, but immediately reformed in their wake. Caw called more and more crows in a ceaseless barrage. Wave after wave smashed through Cynthia Davenport, so fast she barely had time to re-form before the next assault.

Glum swooped past, beak full of flies.

There are too many, Caw, he gasped.

Shimmer was leading the other birds, cutting back and forth. Caw joined them, ripping through air so thick with insects he could hardly breathe. He flapped his wings rapidly, fighting upwards, until he broke through into clean air. With his crow-tongue, he tasted the tang of ozone and the promise of lightning. He wheeled over and let the currents hold him, surveying the battle. Crows flitted like blown–black ash-flakes, burying themselves in the flies, then rising again.

Caw looked about, but he couldn't see Cynthia Davenport anywhere. Had she fled, using her flies as cover? Looking down he was almost sure the insects were fewer than before. The swarm seemed to be collapsing under its own weight, a slick of flies falling in on itself in a huge whirlpool. Caw drew his crows back with a single thought and they lifted up to join him. He stared into the depths of the fly tornado as clear air and the rooftop became visible again below.

His blood turned to ice in his veins.

Standing there was a thing that looked like Cynthia Davenport. But it loomed three times as tall and was growing by the second as more flies poured from the sky across its limbs, clinging to its surface and swelling its size. How was it possible? She must be controlling hundreds of thousands of flies, choreographing each individual flight.

Er... can you *do that?* Shimmer mumbled, hovering beside him.

Caw shook his crow head. He had controlled the flock in his battle against the Spinning Man, but not like that.

The giant shape of the Mother of Flies stood two storeys tall, then lifted weightlessly from the rooftop. The skin and hair were flies, but the contours of her face were the same as ever, the mouth twisted in a smile.

"Behold true power, crow talker!" she said. Her voice came not from her lips, but from her whole body, a strange acoustic mixture of buzzing. Her eyes were black orbs, rolling in their sockets.

She flung a hand in a swatting motion, bashing crows aside like dust motes. Caw sent a wave of birds to attack. They plunged into the black mass of her body, swallowed by flies. Caw waited for them to emerge from the other side, but only half their number smashed free from the insect bulk.

Another giant hand stormed in from his left. Caw folded his wings and dived away, only to see the other massive hand reaching for him, the fingers formed out

263

of thick columns of insects. Angling his beak he stabbed through the solid mass, feeling the flies tangle in his feathers. He tried to flap, but couldn't. The flies blinded him, smothering his beak and paralysing his wings. Their buzzing filled his thoughts, so he was unable to concentrate on anything else. He felt his mental hold on his crow form weakening, and through a chink in the swarm he saw his human hand, so white against the swirling blackness. Then his head broke free – his human head – and he sucked in a lungful of air.

"So there you are!" growled the Mother of Flies.

Caw was entirely human again, gripped in a fly-hand high above the ground. Rain spattered his face. He writhed, but the flies held him, cushioned tightly, compressing his chest. Even through his fear, he marvelled at the strange sensation of tiny bodies pressed against his limbs. Down below he saw dozens of foxes watching him from the rooftop. The Strickhams, Lydia and Selina were there too, staring upwards. Not a single fly remained. All had been conscripted to the service of their mistress.

"Stop fighting, Caw," said Cynthia Davenport. The hand holding Caw gave a further squeeze, making it impossible to breathe. How could creatures so small create such force? "You know, in a way, I was there when your mother died," she said. "My flies watched the Spinning Man kill her." Caw's heart blazed with fury.

"She put up quite a fight, even when the odds were stacked against her." The hand dragged Caw through the air, closer to the fly feral's face. "She was like you, Caw," said the booming voice. "Even at the end, she wasn't ready to give up. Even as his spiders began to consume her."

Caw tried again to break free, straining his arms against the flies, but they hardened against him like concrete. "My mother had more courage than you'll ever know," he said, grimacing. "Even if you kill me, others will stop you."

The giant mouth smiled. "You know, that's almost exactly what she said, before she died."

"And she was *right*!" shouted Caw. "We killed the Spinning Man."

Cynthia Davenport opened her mouth wide. Inside, flies configured themselves into teeth, and a huge rolling ball became her tongue. She began to draw him towards the chasm of her mouth headfirst. From the rooftop below, Caw heard Lydia screaming.

She was going to eat him alive.

The darkness closed over him and all he could hear was the hungry buzzing of flies. There was no way to tell which way was up or down. Insects crowded into his ears and nostrils. He tried to clench his mouth closed, but he could feel their stubborn bodies prising open his lips. His eyes were scrunched so tight they ached.

It couldn't end like this. He thought of his mother

and father dying to protect him. He thought of the crow line who had guarded the Midnight Stone for hundreds of years. He thought of Crumb, and Pip, and all the other ferals who would surely die if the Mother of Flies was victorious. His powerlessness made him furious with himself.

And through the fear and anger came voices.

Where are you?

Is he inside?

What shall we do?

Crow voices, tumbling over each other. Multiplying into a tumult.

Caw sensed their bodies, their wings and beaks and talons. They were waiting for him, waiting for his command.

The first of the flies managed to squeeze into his mouth, leading others. They scrambled across the barrier of his teeth. Caw tried to ignore them and the threat of paralysing panic. He imagined his body set like stone and impervious. He sent out his consciousness as he had done in the Land of the Dead, searching for the crows. He'd need them all.

He almost gagged as flies flooded into the upper reaches of his nose.

He found Shimmer first and his mind enveloped her. Looking down with her eyes he saw the giant shape of Cynthia Davenport. The sky was filled with waiting crows. He latched on to the one nearest to Shimmer, then another. With each crow he gathered to his cause, he felt stronger. His will spread like a net across the flock, and as he possessed them all he drove them in a swirl around the Mother of Flies.

The fly feral twisted, lashing out with her arms. Caw guided the birds with a single twitch of his mind and they followed in a swathe, riding over the limbs that threatened to swat them from the sky. Caw drew more and more birds, until they formed a spinning wall around the Mother of Flies.

The flies had found their way beneath his eyelids. Caw tried to shake his head but there were too many. His eyes began to sting. Others found their way past his teeth and surged into his mouth, crawling over each other to enter his throat.

Caw abandoned his body to their assault, thrusting his entire mind into the crows. In an instant he became thousands of birds.

Now! he cried.

Their wings angled in unison and the tornado around Cynthia Davenport closed in. The crows opened their mouths with a single shriek as they ripped into her fly-flesh, skinning insects away, crunching them in their talons and beaks. Caw focused all his energy on keeping the flock together, keeping their momentum, tightening the circle further. He heard a strange sound of hissing, desperate agony from the depths of the fly giant. She could do nothing to stop the crows eating away at her, a thousand pricks of pain every second. There were too many, on all sides, constantly moving.

Caw saw through his crows' eyes, and all they saw was black. He felt their wings, heavy with insects, his strength sapping fast. At any moment, the sheer weight would drag them down and it would all be in vain. A dim, detached part of his consciousness told him that his body was failing. And that if he died, the crows would be lost too.

He couldn't let it happen.

With his last shred of power, he drove the flock towards her heart.

Chapter 22

Caw lost control. **He heard** a deep rumbling groan of anguish and wondered if it was his own, or if it came from the thunder of the storm. He felt his body falling in fits and starts, caught then released, flipped over this way and that as if he was tumbling through the branches of a thick tree.

Then clear, cold air...

He hit something solid, his head slamming down in a burst of white light. He couldn't breathe and rolled on to his knees, chest heaving for oxygen. His eyes stung so much he could hardly open them. Then from the depths of his guts, a choke ripped through him. He retched helplessly and a throatful of dead flies spattered on to the ground in front of him.

It took him a second to realise he was back on the rooftop.

Cries of agony reverberated across the top of the

building. Caw looked up to see the Mother of Flies still hovering, flailing madly in the sky. He must have fallen from deep inside her. With every wail her form was shrinking as the flies abandoned her. The crows were still attacking, relentlessly tearing at her body. At last she stopped struggling and dropped. A ball of flies smashed into the rooftop and burst away into the night, leaving a human body behind, lying prone on the ground. Cynthia Davenport.

The crows swirled above her, waiting for Caw's command.

Caw found his feet and staggered towards her, drawing the Crow's Beak from his back. He was weak and dizzy, but his anger surged hotly. His hand seemed to have a will of its own as it raised the blade above her body. Caw longed to bring it down, stabbing her through her black heart.

But he paused. Selina's mother lay beneath him, curled and unconscious. Her expensive suit was torn to pieces, and her skin was covered in bleeding cuts from the crows' attack. In places her hair had been ripped from her scalp.

Footsteps came running across the rooftop.

"Mum?" said Selina. She dropped beside Cynthia Davenport, her face wet with tears.

Caw's anger left him in a rush. However cruel and evil the fly feral was, she was still a mother. He let the

Crow's Beak fall limp in his hand. He couldn't make Selina an orphan like himself.

Mrs Strickham approached, leading her foxes. For a moment Caw wondered what she would do, but she merely put two fingers to the throat of the Mother of Flies.

"She's alive," she said. "Just." Caw couldn't tell whether she was happy or sad.

Mr Strickham was on his phone. "... yes, that's right. The top of Verona Tower. The *rooftop*, yes... No, it's the Commissioner who's injured. Send all the men you can."

Lydia reached Caw's side. "Are you all right?" she asked.

Caw staggered back a little, leaning his weight on her. "I think so," he said. He glanced up at the crows still massed in the sky. "Thanks to them."

Shimmer and Glum glided down and joined them.

I'm getting too old for this, said Glum.

Selina looked up from her mother. "Is she going to be all right?"

Hopefully not, muttered Shimmer.

"There's help coming," said Mr Strickham. "They'll do what they can, but... she'll have to be placed in custody, you know that? After all she's done..."

Selina nodded. Her face was deathly pale. She tried to stand, but her leg gave way beneath her. Caw rushed to catch her, but didn't get there in time. She crumpled on top of her mother and the Midnight Stone fell from her hand, gleaming softly.

"Selina?" Caw said.

Her eyes closed and she gave no answer. Looking down as he cradled her head, Caw saw that her leg was soaked with blood. "Selina?" he said again. "Hold on."

In the distance, an ambulance siren wailed through the night.

In the afternoon light of the next day, Caw watched the city swish by through Mr Strickham's car window. His eyes kept threatening to close, and his body was bruised and aching, but it was a good sort of exhaustion. After the storm of the previous night, everything looked a little cleaner. Normal people were going about their business, striding to their jobs, holding hands on the pavements, drinking in cafés. No one knew how close Blackstone had come to catastrophe just a few hours before.

And no one, Caw was sure, noticed that three crows were keeping pace with the car as it made its way through the city. Glum, Shimmer and Screech flitted in and out of his line of sight.

"Are you OK?" asked Lydia, who was sitting beside him.

"Just thinking," he said, "how it only takes a few evil people to bring a city to its knees."

"Only a few good people to save it too," said Lydia, smiling.

"And a few thousand crows."

"We're nearly there," said Mr Strickham from the driver's seat, as they turned a corner towards the abandoned zoo. "Lydia and I will wait outside."

"Er... I don't think so!" said Lydia.

"Sweetheart..." began her father.

"Dad, I'm going in," she said.

They pulled up at the same zoo gates where Chen had dropped them the day before. Velma Strickham was already there, foxes gathered beside her. She had come ahead to spread word of what had happened. It had taken Lydia's father most of the morning at the council offices, but after a lot of discussion he'd been reinstated as governor of the prison and his first act had been to get the innocent ferals released – easy, since the city had no record of their arrest.

Cynthia Davenport had been taken away in a straitjacket, raving about flies and crows.

As they got out of the car Caw noticed that Mr Strickham was staying inside. His wife gave him a strained look.

"Dad, please," said Lydia through the open window.

"This is none of our business," he said, hands still on the wheel and looking straight ahead.

"How can you say that?" Lydia replied. "After everything that's happened?"

Mr Strickham turned to her. "We need to put it behind us," he said. "Get back to being a normal family."

Lydia sighed. "Dad, we're *not* a normal family. Mum's a feral. That means one day I—"

"Enough!" he snapped. "I can't stop you going in there, but I want nothing more to do with those people."

Lydia turned away, close to tears, and joined Caw and her mother. Velma Strickham put her arm around her daughter.

Caw shivered. It was strange being back here, where the Mother of Flies had laid her ambush.

"You must come over for dinner soon," Mrs Strickham said to him.

"Will Mr Strickham be OK with that?" Caw asked.

Mrs Strickham shrugged. "He'll have to be. We all need to adapt. Perhaps you and I can even practise together in the park. I wouldn't mind you teaching me a few tricks."

Caw was almost speechless. Was Velma Strickham – the fox feral of Blackstone – *really* asking him for advice?

"Of course, if you're too busy..." she continued.

"No. No!" said Caw. "It would be an honour. If you... I mean, whenever."

"Come on," said Lydia smiling and taking his hand. "You're making *me* embarrassed."

Caw's heart lifted as they entered the old penguin enclosure and he saw Crumb and Pip waiting side by side. Crumb was feeding bits of bread to his birds.

"You're here!" Caw said, running up to hug them both. But as he drew close, his footsteps slowed. Crumb looked serious, and Pip stared at the floor. Perhaps they were still angry about being locked up. They had every right to be.

"You look like a wreck," said Crumb gruffly.

Caw shrugged. His jacket was ripped in places from the eagle's talons and his trousers were streaked with dirt from the roof. "It was a long night."

"You should have tried spending it in a cold jail cell with twenty other ferals and no working toilet."

Caw cleared his throat. "Look, I'm sorry. I..."

Crumb's face broke into a smile and he opened his arms. "Come here, kid."

Relief rushed through Caw as he embraced Crumb. After Crumb had let him go, he took Caw by both shoulders. "I'm so proud of you, Caw," he said. "We heard about what you did on the rooftop."

"But tell us in your own words," said Pip, practically jumping up and down. "We heard you controlled ten thousand crows!"

Caw blushed. "I thought I'd never see either of you again," he said. "When we learned what the Mother of Flies was planning, creating new ferals, I thought she'd..." A wave of sickness passed over him as he imagined what might have been.

"A few hours in prison, that was all we suffered," said

Crumb. "Some had it worse – at least Pip's mice could sneak into the kitchens and steal us extra food."

Pip was smiling shyly. "So, did you really take on the Mother of Flies on your own?"

Excuse me! said Screech, flapping.

The other crows joined in the protest, squawking madly.

"I might have had a little help," said Caw smiling. "And I wouldn't have stood a chance without all the training, of course."

Crumb gave him a punch on the shoulder and Caw winced.

"Something tells me you're being modest," said the pigeon feral. "Velma told us what you did. I just wish I could have seen that woman get what she deserved. Her daughter too."

As the pain from Caw's shoulder receded, a deeper pain surfaced at the thought of Selina. He wanted to change the subject.

"Listen," he said. "I've been thinking... about the church."

Pip looked worried. "You are coming back, aren't you?"

Caw smiled. "Well, that's what I've been wondering. I actually have a house, you know? And it doesn't have a hole in the roof."

A few of the scattered pigeons warbled in protest,

until Crumb held out a finger. "Quiet, you lot. He didn't mean it like that."

"So how about it?" said Caw.

Crumb's mouth turned down. "Well, if you'd prefer to live there, I can't stop you..."

"No!" said Caw. "Not just me – all three of us. You and Pip too. I mean, it needs a bit of work, but..."

Crumb rocked back on his heels. "What? Me? In a real house?"

"Oh, *please* can we?" said Pip, tugging at his arm. "Think of it! Bedrooms, a kitchen, a working toilet. It'll be like we're a real family."

Crumb hesitated a moment more, before smiling broadly. "When you put it like that... well, we accept!"

A wolf prowled into the enclosure, then lay in a patch of sun. Racklen came in next, pushing Madeleine the squirrel feral in her wheelchair. Caw was glad to see her again and she smiled warmly at him. Other ferals followed. Caw recognised them from the last zoo visit, but there were more besides. Soon the enclosure was thronging with men, women and children, young and old. Ali the bee feral was dressed in his dark business suit as always, looking like he'd just stepped out of his office for lunch. Birds fluttered overhead and came to rest on the railings. Caw noticed that a single cat was sitting beside a noticeboard – Freddie. Caw scanned the faces of the assembled ferals, but Felix Quaker was not among them.

"So where is she now?" growled Racklen. "Where's the Mother of Flies?"

Velma Strickham held up a hand to placate the wolf feral. "She's been taken to the mental hospital on the other side of Blackstone."

"The hospital!" said Racklen. "She should be brought here, to face feral justice."

"She's no threat now," said Mrs Strickham. "She strained her powers too far in trying to defeat Caw and now her bond with the flies has been broken. The police rounded up the animals she'd kept in her apartment. They're trying to track down the helicopter and find the escaped prisoners now. Meanwhile, my husband is having her monitored twenty-four hours a day under a maximum security guard."

"Your husband?" said Ali. "A non feral? What does he know?"

"He has seen what she's capable of," said Mrs Strickham. "She will not harm anyone again."

The ferals burst into discontented mutterings.

"That's not good enough," said Racklen, advancing on Lydia's mother. Her foxes snarled and stood in his path and his wolf's hackles rose menacingly. "Turn her over to us," he said. "We'll deal with her. This city won't be safe while she breathes its air."

"We can't just kill her," interrupted Caw.

"She was ready to kill all of *us*!" said the wolf feral.

"But we're better than her," Caw said.

The mutterings slowly died down, but still people didn't look happy.

"Caw has a grievance against Cynthia Davenport as great as any of us," said Mrs Strickham. "If he can control his desire for vengeance, then so can we."

Caw glanced at Mrs Strickham, then at Lydia. Even they didn't know how close he had come in his heart to killing the Mother of Flies. He remembered the rush of anger and the feeling of the Crow's Beak ready to deliver a fatal blow. And he knew what had stopped him wasn't just the fact that she was defenceless. It was Selina. He couldn't have deprived her of her mother. When she woke up – *if* she ever did – he didn't want it to be to the news that she too was an orphan. That was the misery the Spinning Man had inflicted on him, and he wouldn't inflict it on anyone else.

Caw leant over and murmured to Velma Strickham.

"I need to go to the hospital," he said.

Chapter 23

Blackstone General Hospital was a grim and forbidding complex in the south of the city. Chen dropped Caw and Lydia in front of the main building and told them that he'd be waiting in the car park. Caw asked his crows to wait outside too.

"Birds aren't allowed in hospitals," he said.

That's prejudice, that is, Glum grumbled.

As they headed for the hospital entrance, Chen called after them. "Hey, Caw," he said. "Thank you. For everything. For saving us."

Caw blushed and turned away.

"You'll have to get used to that, you know," muttered Lydia. "You're a feral hero now."

Caw grinned, until he remembered why they were here. "I hope she's OK."

Lydia's smile dropped too, but she said nothing. Caw

wondered how she really felt about the daughter of the Mother of Flies.

"Are you family?" asked the receptionist, when they asked for Selina Davenport at the desk.

"No," said Caw. "She's a friend of ours."

"I'm afraid only family can—"

"She doesn't have any," said Lydia. "Her dad's gone and her mum's in a mental hospital."

"Oh, right," said the receptionist, looking embarrassed. "Let me see what I can do."

She made a quick phone call, then directed them to the juvenile ward.

The corridors were too bright for Caw's liking and he caught a few nurses throwing strange glances at his torn black clothes. They reached the ward at last and saw the curtain had been pulled across the glass screen so it was impossible to see inside. Fearing the worst, Caw opened the door.

There was only a single bed inside and the window blinds were closed as well, casting the room in a half-light. Selina Davenport was propped up against several pillows, wearing a hospital gown. A nurse was checking her drip.

"Oh, hello," said the nurse. "Reception said you were on your way. Still unresponsive, I'm afraid."

Tubes and wires trailed from both of Selina's arms

and the gunshot wound on her leg was bandaged heavily. Her eyes were closed. Machines bleeped out a regular, slow heartbeat.

"Do you know what's wrong with her?" asked Caw.

The nurse looked for a long time at Selina's face, so peaceful. "The doctors are trying to work it out. There's some sort of toxin in her blood, an infection, but they're struggling to identify it. Very odd for a gunshot wound."

The nurse made some notes on a clipboard at the end of the bed. "She's certainly a fighter. I hope there's some good news soon." Tucking away the pen, the nurse left the room, closing the door and leaving them alone.

Lydia and Caw approached the sick girl in the bed.

"I didn't trust her for a long time," Lydia said, "but I guess she proved herself in the end."

Caw sat beside the bed. Selina's face looked slightly swollen, and her eyelids were a pale and sickly lilac.

"It wasn't her fault who her mother is," he said. "Selina?" he added in a whisper.

Nothing.

The door clicked again and he looked up, expecting to see another member of the medical staff. But it was a man dressed in orange corduroy trousers and a vivid purple jacket.

"Felix!" gasped Lydia.

Quaker's eyes travelled quickly over Selina and Lydia,

to Caw, then to his own feet. "Am I disturbing you?" he asked.

Caw felt a surge of anger at Quaker, for not telling him the truth about the Midnight Stone sooner – but he managed to fight it down. "Come in," he said.

Quaker touched his moustache nervously, twisting the ends. "I wanted to apologise," he said quietly.

Caw couldn't think what to say, so he settled for, "Where have you been?"

Quaker shrugged. "Cats always find a hiding place," he replied.

He edged into the room. Caw noticed that Lydia was glaring coldly at him.

"I heard what happened on the rooftop," said the cat feral. "I even sent Freddie to the meeting today, though I didn't come myself."

"Why not?" said Lydia fiercely. "Afraid some might not take kindly to a coward in their midst?"

Quaker swallowed, wringing his hands. "You're quite right, my girl. I have an acute survival instinct. Call it cowardice if you will. I knew of the Midnight Stone, and of the lengths the Mother of Flies would go to in order to possess it. I am not a fighter. Not like the Carmichaels."

"If that's your idea of an apology," said Lydia, "you probably shouldn't have bothered."

Quaker nodded meekly and started to turn.

"No, wait," said Caw. "I want to know – how did you

find out about the Midnight Stone? In the time of Black Corvus, all the ferals signed a pact to die with the secret. Did the cat ferals break the pledge?"

Quaker shook his head. "It wasn't like that," he said. "Never underestimate the tenacity of a historian."

Caw frowned. Quaker reached into his jacket and took out a small scroll of parchment. As the cat feral unrolled it, Caw recognised it from the memory in Bootlace's cavern. The writing was faded and so squiggly Caw couldn't decipher the letters, but one signature scrawled at the base stood out. He took the parchment and brought it closer to his eyes.

Black Corvus.

"It's the pledge of secrecy!" he said.

Quaker smiled weakly. "I had this in my collection for years," he said. "Never knew if it was really genuine, but I suspected."

Caw frowned. There was a piece of this puzzle that didn't fit. He remembered the other vision in Bootlace's lair, the one in which his mother had brought the stone to Bootlace for protection. Her words were still so clear and fresh.

The spider feral has learnt of its existence.

But how? Unless...

His blood went cold.

"Felix," he said, "did you tell the Spinning Man about the Midnight Stone?"

Felix straightened proudly. "I certainly did not!" he said. "I may not be the bravest feral in Blackstone, but I am no traitor!"

"Sorry," said Caw. "I shouldn't have..."

"No, no," said Quaker. "I understand why you might say that. The truth is, I don't know how he found out. If I had known, I would have warned your mother he was coming for her. She was... a good woman."

He lowered his head and silence fell over the room, broken only by the sound of the life-support machines.

"I buried them, you know," mumbled the old man, lifting his head. Tears were welling in his eyes.

"What?" said Caw.

"It was me who found your parents," said Quaker. "Well, the cats did. I took their bodies to the cemetery and dug their graves myself. Right beside Henry Wythe."

Caw felt as though his heart was struggling to beat. "Thank you," he said hoarsely. "And for the message on Freddie's collar. We wouldn't have found Bootlace without your help."

Quaker nodded briskly, wiped his eyes and sniffed, then seemed to notice Selina properly for the first time since entering the room. "And this is her daughter, is it?" he asked. "The heiress to the fly line."

Caw walked to the end of the bed and tugged out the clipboard. He scanned the writing, but most of the long words meant nothing to him. "They say they don't know what's wrong with her. Some sort of poison in her blood."

Quaker twitched, suddenly alert. "Poison? I thought she was shot?"

"She was," said Lydia.

Quaker frowned. "Well, medicine isn't my field, I'm afraid." He seemed back to his old self. "I will leave you, if I may. My house is in need of some care after the barbarities of our city's constabulary."

"Of course," said Caw.

"Goodbye, Felix," said Lydia, rolling her eyes behind his back.

"Farewell," said the cat feral. He spun on his heel and left.

When he'd closed the door, Lydia came to Caw's side and touched his arm. "Are you OK?" she said. "Y'know, about your parents?"

Caw shrugged. "It was a long time ago, wasn't it?"

Lydia smiled softly.

"Can you give me a moment alone?" he asked.

Lydia hesitated for just a second before nodding. "I'll see you outside."

After she had gone, Caw eased his aching body into the chair beside Selina's bed.

It *was* a long time ago. He remembered nothing of his parents when they were alive and even the memory of meeting them in the Land of the Dead was fading like a photograph bleached by the sun. But he could never forget the sacrifice they'd made so that he could live. And he would never take lightly the feral powers handed down to him. If they were watching him now, he knew they'd both be proud.

Caw let his hand rest over his pocket where the Midnight Stone remained, wrapped in his handkerchief. He wouldn't touch it again, and he wouldn't let anyone else touch it either. The crow line had not failed. *He* had not failed the pledge that Black Corvus had made hundreds of years before.

He looked at Selina, lying as still as a corpse in the bed. A victim of the war between the ferals, as so many had been before her. There would be more too, he realised. The Spinning Man was dead, the Mother of Flies had lost her creatures and would never see freedom again. But Crumb was right – evil rested, yet never died. And when it woke again, Caw and his crows would be ready to face it.

He placed his hand over Selina's.

"I'm sorry," he said quietly.

The only answer was the soft electronic bleep of her heartbeat.